A SHOCKING
PROPOSAL
IN SICILY

A SHOCKING PROPOSAL IN SICILY

RACHAEL THOMAS

MILLS & BOON

First published in Great Britain 2019
by Mills & Boon, an imprint of HarperCollins*Publishers*
1 London Bridge Street, London, SE1 9GF

Large Print edition 2020

© 2019 Rachael Thomas

ISBN: 978-0-263-08919-6

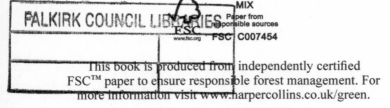

Printed and bound in Great Britain
by CPI Group (UK) Ltd, Croydon, CR0 4YY

For the fantastic group of adventurers I trekked across the Sahara Desert with in November 2018, raising funds for many charities. Especially 'The Desert Girls'—Sohere, Hanna, Rowena, Danni and Pippa—with whom I shared the most basic tent. The whole week was an awesome and unforgettable adventure!

PROLOGUE

SHE'D HAD HER FREEDOM. Freedom which now needed to be paid for. The last five years of resisting the urge to fulfil the archaic traditions of her country counted for nothing. Her duty to Ardu Safra could no longer be ignored. Or avoided.

Kaliana Benhamed stood outside her father's office. She knew exactly why he'd demanded she return from London. From the new life she'd carved for herself after the tragedy of five years ago. Why he'd insisted she leave a job she loved, as campaign manager for Charity Resources. It didn't concern him she'd have to say goodbye to Claire, a friend who knew everything about her but still treated her like an everyday girl. With that one command, her father had all but brought her world crashing down around her, leaving her no option but to return to her homeland and face him. Face her duty.

Kaliana stood taller, taking a deep breath, desperate to quell the churning of her stomach, her heart pounding hard and fast at the thought of the discussion to come. She swallowed down the nerves she couldn't allow her father to see. She was a different woman from the one who'd left Ardu Safra after the nightmare of losing the man she'd loved. Since then, she'd found her independence and happiness. She'd pushed aside her dreams of love and happy ever afters. Made a new life for herself. A life she wasn't about to relinquish easily.

Not even to her father, ruler of Ardu Safra, a small desert kingdom on the north-eastern edge of the African continent. He'd been a strict father, but fair. Would he really force her to do the one thing she didn't want to do? Would he force her to accept a man he'd selected, as her husband? After everything she'd endured?

She closed her eyes briefly, sending up one last prayer for the strength to do this, wishing her mother had a more modern outlook on life. Wishing she would stand up for her only child. But those wishes were futile. Her mother was kind and loving, but of a very different era.

Kaliana tried to shake the tension from her shoulders as she gave the command to the guards, always stationed around the palace, to admit her to her father's office.

The big doors swung wide and she walked across the vastness of the marble floor to the ornate desk at the far end of the room. Her father looked up from his work, watching her intently. Did he notice how different she was? How strong? How ready she was to do battle with him? To fight for her right to be a modern woman in a modern world?

She knew she had to marry and when that happened she wanted to drag the kingdom of Ardu Safra into the twenty-first century. For the people of the small kingdom as much as for herself. But she wasn't ready yet.

'Kaliana.' His voice was cool. Distant. As if he was addressing one of his aides, not his daughter. His only child. And that was the core of her problem. She was the only heir of Ardu Safra. 'At last you return to your country.'

The reproach in his voice bounced round the vastness of the ornate office, mirroring itself in his dark, watchful eyes. Warning her he wasn't in the mood for her wilfulness, as he often called it.

'You didn't leave me much choice.' Kaliana stopped a short distance from her father's desk, satisfaction racing through her as he took in, with annoyance, her shorter hair. She loved the long bob style she'd opted for as part of the new Kaliana. Already she could feel her hackles rise, her indignation at the injustice surging to the fore. She battled to keep it contained. Keep it from her father. 'You made it clear that my coming was not a request, Father, but a demand.'

The shock of receiving the curt email directly from her father still hadn't subsided. Neither had the knowledge that the life she'd built herself was in serious danger. She was expected to marry and, at twenty-five, she was acutely aware he considered that duty well overdue.

She'd stepped outside the life of Kaliana Benhamed, Princess of Ardu Safra, for five years and now it was time to go back to the life her title demanded. It was time to do the duty she'd hoped she'd never have to do. Live the life she'd tried to be free of.

'What are you wearing?' His gaze took in her fitted navy skirt and white blouse, teamed with heeled shoes. Her chosen clothes for her new work life. He wouldn't approve of them, just as her traditionally brought-up mother didn't. Kaliana was a big disappointment to her parents in many ways.

'This is who I am now, Father.' She lifted her chin defiantly as he stared at her, his annoyance that she'd turned her back so blatantly on her country vividly clear on his face. Once again it was clear she was a total disappointment to him. The daughter who'd brought shame to him. To the country. 'Whatever it is you want of me, this is who I am now.'

He stood up quickly, his heavy chair scraping noisily on the marble floor. Anger burned in his eyes as he leant on the desk. 'What I want is for you to do your duty.'

Kaliana wanted to step back from his fury. 'My duty, Father?' she asked, in a voice so light it didn't even sound like her own. But to show her fear to him, her fear of what he now expected her to do, would be to hand him the ace card. Give him all the power.

And it was a power she'd slowly and bit by bit taken from him over the last five years as her new life had proved she could succeed without the title of Princess Kaliana of Ardu Safra. She'd got herself a managerial job, a place to live and friends she could count on without disclosing her royal title. Only Claire knew the truth. To her employer, her colleagues and friends, she was simply Kaliana Benhamed. And the fact she'd achieved all that irritated her father far more than he let on.

'Marriage.' He hurled the word she least wanted to hear at her. 'Marriage is your duty, Kaliana. Your duty as Princess to the kingdom of Ardu Safra. Your duty as my daughter and only heir.'

She clenched her hands tightly, her nails digging into the sweaty palms. 'Not in the life I now lead, Father.'

'The life you now lead?' Her father's voice lowered with disappointment, the scowl on his face full of annoyance and frustration. She was only making this worse. Making it harder for herself. Making him angrier. 'I've allowed you to indulge in that fancy long enough.'

She stepped forward, her own frustration making her reckless. 'It's not a fancy, Father, it's my life now. One I needed to make for myself.'

He sighed slowly and looked at her, his expression softening very slightly, making her think of the father he'd been when she was younger. The father who'd loved her even though she hadn't been born a son. The father who had been more relaxed—until the burden of inheriting and ruling a financially struggling and small kingdom had snatched that man away. 'I understand why you needed to go. That's why I said nothing when you turned your back on the lifestyle your title could have brought you.'

'Then you will understand why I can't marry. Not ever.'

'It's not that simple, Kaliana. Our kingdom is in jeopardy. Our people too. The only way out of it is for you to marry.' The resignation in his voice shocked her. The angry ruler of moments ago had gone. The man she'd loved as a carefree child had returned. It was that man who tugged on her conscience.

'And who will I marry, Father? Alif, the man I loved, the man you were perfectly happy for me to marry, died—remember?' A stab of pain shot through her as she recalled being told her fiancé had been killed in a tragic helicopter crash just weeks before their wedding.

'Nassif has asked for your hand in marriage.' Her father's words cut savagely through that memory.

'Nassif?' Kaliana couldn't believe she was hearing right. How could he do this to her?

How could her father even think she would marry anyone? But Nassif?

'Alif's uncle? Alif's cruel and spiteful uncle? You can't mean that?' Her voice was a strangled cry of pain and despair. Her throat had gone dry, as if she'd walked all day in the heat of the desert and not taken one sip of water. Her head spun and she dragged in rapid deep breaths, desperate to regain control of herself and this conversation. 'I can't. I. Can't.'

'Marriage to Nassif will unite our countries, just as they should have been five years ago, if you'd married Alif.' Her father sat once again behind his desk, the formidable ruler he'd become slipping back into place. The glimpse of the father she'd known long ago, gone. Or was it just her wishful thinking? She'd foolishly been hoping her father would be pleased to see her after five years. How wrong could she be?

Kaliana's knees weakened and she wished she could slump to the floor as past hurt, past pain and heartache collided with the panic of what her father had planned. What he expected her to do without question. 'But Nassif is so much older than me.'

'That is true,' he said slowly, his response to her objection so obviously rehearsed. 'Now that his wife has passed away, he wants to make you his wife.'

Kaliana backed away, needing the roar of panic in her head to stop, needing the wild spinning of her mind to cease. 'No. I will not marry him.'

Sweat prickled on her forehead. Nausea rose and the need to turn and run became almost irresistible. But she couldn't run. Somewhere deep inside her, the duty her mother had implanted so innocuously into her from a young age resurfaced. Took over.

She wanted to run. But she couldn't. She had a duty to do. Duty to her family. Her kingdom.

Deep down, she'd always known her father had allowed her time away, allowed her time to heal the pain of her broken heart. But now that reprieve was over. It was time for her to do the right thing. Do the duty she'd been born to.

But marriage to Nassif? She shivered with sickening revulsion. Marriage to anyone would be bad enough, but to her late fiancé's vile uncle? Unthinkable.

Her father watched her without saying anything. He didn't even flinch when, with a great shuddering breath that could lead to tears if she let it, she looked at him. Imploring him to understand. Imploring him to tell her he'd find someone else.

Someone else. The words wandered around her mind like mist on an autumn morning in London, shrouding all other thoughts. What if she did marry someone else?

Spurred on by the idea, the desperate thought that this was the solution, she moved back towards him. 'I can't marry Nassif, Father.'

'Ardu Safra is facing financial ruin. Whilst you have been in London things have become very bad here.'

'Why didn't you tell me?'

'It is for me to deal with. I was counting on your marriage to Alif to make things right.' The sharpness of his words only just hid his panic, the seriousness of the situation.

'There were problems even then?' she asked, saddened to think she'd been happy and free in London, while her mother and father had carried this burden.

'Yes. And now I must ask that you make a marriage with Nassif.' His voice had hardened. Was that to hide his shame that things had got so bad in the country he ruled? Guilt raced through her, forming a potent cocktail, mixing with her fear. A cocktail that made her almost physically sick.

'Father, no. Not Nassif.'

'He is a very wealthy man.' Her father looked at her, no longer the strong ruler but a man who looked broken and defeated. A man who was depending on her. Her heart wrenched. 'And he is willing to invest in Ardu Safra.'

She shook her head in protest, but the straight line of her father's mouth warned her it was in vain.

'Your marriage will bring the finances you should have brought with your marriage five years ago.' She knew that gritty determination in his voice. He would get what he wanted. One way or another. And he wanted to save Ardu Safra by marrying her off to a wealthy man.

But did that man have to be Nassif?

A solution barged into her mind, making any further words almost impossible. Her heart thudded loudly. Dare she risk telling him? Risk his anger? And, worst of all, his disapproval of her. 'No. I can't do it.'

'Imagine the shame your mother will face.' He believed he held the ace cards, but she wouldn't allow him to emotionally blackmail her. He wouldn't use the close relationship she and her mother had always shared. He wouldn't do that to her any more.

'This isn't about Mother,' she said flatly, glaring at him, that wilful streak of hers beginning to take over as the solution to her problem grew in possibility. Like the sun as it rose over the mountains of the desert. Becoming bigger and stronger with each passing minute.

'And the people of Ardu Safra? Will you stand by and allow them to wallow in poverty and hunger because you won't do your duty? Because you won't make a marriage to bring wealth back to our kingdom?'

Damn it, he did hold the ace cards. All of them. And he played them well. Too well.

'Don't, Father,' she snapped.

'How will your charities view you when they know who you really are? That you turned your back on the country of your birth? Its people?' He stood once more, realising she was retreating, on the verge of accepting defeat. His threat to reveal her true identity, even though he'd helped her keep it secret, all he needed to use.

'That's not fair.' How had she thought he was a fair man?

'You will *have* to marry someone, Kaliana. A man with great wealth. A man able to rule by your side when the time comes.' He paused, letting the image of her future permeate her mind. 'This is your country. Your people.'

Marry someone. That was what he'd said. Again, the other less hideous option rushed into her mind. That was it. She would find her own husband.

'Then I will find someone else.' The words tumbled out in a panic and she knew she was in danger of losing the control she was fighting to keep on her emotions. 'I will find a man to marry who can bring the finances needed to Ardu Safra.'

Her father looked at her, scowling, but before he could shut down her idea she spoke again. 'I cannot and will not marry Nassif.'

She expected him to be angry. Braced herself for his wrath, but it didn't come. He looked as stunned as she felt.

He shook his head in disbelief. 'You really think you can find a man, one wealthier than Nassif, willing to marry you and take on the demands of being husband to a princess?'

'Yes, Father, I do.' Now her panic changed direction. How could she ever achieve that?

'Very well, I will prepare for a wedding.'

'What?'

'On the day of your twenty-sixth birthday you will be married.'

'But that's…' She paused to calculate, her mind too numb to function. 'October. The beginning of October. Only four months away.'

He nodded solemnly. She wanted to rail against him, but he'd changed. There was something different about him. Something that tugged mercilessly at her heartstrings. Something that once again hinted that the father she'd loved as a child, the man she wished he could be, lingered beneath his tough exterior.

But she wasn't about to let go of the chance he'd given her. 'And if I haven't found a husband by then?' Inside she was a wild rush of panic. She could do this. She *had* to do this.

'You have until September,' her father solemnly said. 'Find a suitable husband by then or marry Nassif on your twenty-sixth birthday.'

CHAPTER ONE

Early June

RAFFAELE CASELLA COULD hardly control his frustration. Even as he'd flown back from Sicily to London, he hadn't been able to halt the flow of anger. The irritation. His father, alarmingly calm after his cancer diagnosis, had hammered home the stark reality of the situation the family was now in.

The Casella name could end. And with it the possession of land and wealth which had been handed from one Casella generation to the next. With appalling timing, his twin brother, Enzo, had chosen that very day to admit his marriage to Emma was in jeopardy, after a fertility test had proved he was unable to father children—Casella heirs. His father had panicked, turning immediately to Rafe, putting the duty of providing the next generation squarely on his shoulders. Now he was the only one who could ensure the Casella land and wealth stayed exactly that.

Rafe had fought to control his anger, his shock, throughout the discussion with his father and Enzo. Reminding himself the old man was ill, holding it all in, thinking instead of the father he'd spent his life trying to please, but failing at every turn. Enzo, the first-born twin, was the son who had always achieved that honour, even when he'd betrayed Rafe in the most heartless way, tearing apart a family already living under the cloud of tragedy.

The Casella name would end if he, the second-born twin, the spare heir, didn't marry and have children. The biggest crisis the Casella family had faced for three generations now loomed over them.

Rafe was in the spotlight, its brightness harsh and unyielding. Inescapable. He was the only one who could save the Casella name, and with it the family fortune. Pressure bore down on him. His future was mapped out, demanding he take a route that involved a marriage he'd never intended to make. Children—or, more precisely, a son to continue the Casella name—something he'd never wanted.

He had no choice. Either that or stand by and watch their cousin Serafina and her greedy husband, Giovanni Romano, take everything, ending the Casella dynasty.

Rafe couldn't allow that. Not when part of that dynasty was the one piece of land which meant more to him than anything else. His mother's land. The place he and Enzo, along with childhood friend Franco, had once played happily. It was a place full of memories of his mother. Memories he'd treasured since her death when he and Enzo had been only teenagers. For those olive groves alone, Rafe would do anything. Even marry. Even become a father. It was far more than ensuring nobody else, other than a Casella, owned Pietra Bianca. For Rafe it was about keeping his mother's memory alive.

The thought of Giovanni at the ancient olive grove slammed into Rafe as he ordered a second whisky. A surge of anger raced through him, almost blocking out the subtle tones of the gentle piano music weaving through the bar of the exclusive London hotel.

There was no way Giovanni Romano was having anything to do with Pietra Bianca.

Rafe swigged the fiery liquid back and banged the empty glass down on the bar. During the last heated words he and his brother had shared, Enzo had made it clear that, despite everything that had gone on between them, he expected Rafe to step up. Expected him to save the Casella fortune. Proving his twin was as mercenary, as motivated by wealth, as their father.

'Damn you, Father,' Rafe muttered as he glared at the offensively empty glass. 'And damn you, Enzo.'

Rafe pushed his hands through his hair as he thought of Serafina and Giovanni claiming the Casella fortune. No. That could never happen. Irritation tipped over to anger and Rafe called over the bartender, watching him with narrowed eyes, his thoughts elsewhere, as another glass of whisky was poured.

Picking up the glass, Rafe raised it to his

reflection in the mirrors behind the bar. To his future. Marriage. Fatherhood. The things he'd never wanted, now his only option.

Rafe looked down into the amber liquid in the crystal tumbler, still questioning the wisdom of marriage. The ice-cold shock which had hit him as his father had made his expectations clear was still frozen inside him, the whisky unable to thaw it.

His father had always considered Enzo the true heir, expecting his first-born son to marry, produce the new generation and claim it all. Rafe was, as always, merely the back-up plan. An extra card in his hand.

A card he was now forced to play after Enzo's marriage was crashing on the rocks so spectacularly. Divorce seemed the only option. Poor Emma. Rafe tried to push the sympathy away. She might have been his first love, but she was now Enzo's wife. Enzo and Emma's betrayal had gone far deeper than just killing his love for her.

Rafe swirled the whisky in the glass, brooding into it as if it held the answers to the nightmare he now lived. He had no wish for marriage. No need for emotional complications. How was he to find himself a wife? And one that would bring the kind of prestigious advantages to the marriage he required and the son the Casella family required? Did he really have such little choice that he had to accept a marriage deal arranged by his father?

Anger chased the whisky through his body. Was he to parade himself like a stud horse? That stung his male pride as much as being the standby heir.

'Champagne.' The husky voice of the woman joining him at the bar caught his attention, dragging him from his despair, her accent intriguing him as she made her demand to the bartender. Despite the weight of his problems, he was captivated in a way he hadn't been for a long time.

Rafe studied her in the mirrors behind the bar and, despite the rows of optics, saw the woman was as attractive as her voice. There was an air of sophistication about her. She radiated confidence, drew him ever closer. Making him want more than a curious glance in the mirror. Making him want to get to know her. Effectively sealing his fate.

Attraction surged through him and he reluctantly admitted he'd go as far as to say she was the sexiest woman he'd seen in a long time. She was tall and slender, wearing a tight-fitting pale gold silk blouse, sleeves folded up past her elbows and open low at the front. Her dark shoulder-length hair was pulled back away from her face, accentuating her vivid brown eyes, her brown eye make-up making them appear as black as coal. Her full lips were pressed together into a sulky but sexy pout.

She was utterly gorgeous.

Watching her shouldn't have turned him on, but it did. A lick of hot lust, reminding him just how long it had been since he'd lost himself in the oblivion of a beautiful woman, fired through him. It would also be something he'd never be able to do again once he married. His marriage might not be for love, or any kind of sentiment, but his morals wouldn't allow for such betrayal as infidelity.

He knew how that felt. All too well.

Rafe nodded to the bartender, who swiftly brought over two glasses and a bottle of champagne, placing them on the bar between him and the woman. With a quick glance at the label, Rafe satisfied himself his usual standards had been catered for with nothing but the best and moved closer to the sexy woman.

'I don't recall inviting you to join me.' She turned, leaning one slender arm on the bar, cutting off any polite introductions he could have made as she glared up at him. That lick of lust just became a savage kick.

He conjured up an image of the kind of woman his father might suggest as a suitable wife and knew she'd never be a match to this sassy, sophisticated woman before him. He took in the brunette's long bronzed legs, the tight-fitting skirt skimming above her knees and the sexy gold sandals on delicate feet with red painted nails.

This woman oozed confidence. She was strong. Independent. And, with a body like that, she would fill his nights with hot pleasure. There was no way a woman like her would agree to a marriage purely for convenience.

This was a woman who undoubtedly played as hard as she worked. Exactly the kind of woman he was drawn to. He knew instinctively this woman would match him in every way.

'I think you will find it is you who is being invited to join me,' he taunted. Sparks of sexy annoyance shot out at him from her eyes, sending that savage lust roaring straight to his groin. He clenched his jaw against the kind of need he hadn't felt for a long time. The kind of need that right now would chase away the shock of all he'd discovered. All he must do.

'And how do you come to that conclusion? You were very clearly drinking whisky when I arrived,' she goaded him, leaning her head to one side, her diamond earrings sparkling and winking at him.

He smiled. She'd noticed. Noticed him. 'That is true.'

'I was the one who ordered champagne.' Her accent deepened. He'd never met a woman like this. For the last six years he'd consciously avoided complicating his life with female company. He'd used the alternative energy business he'd worked hard to set up, instead of joining his father and Enzo in the family business, to keep him from his homeland. Sicily held too many bad memories. The kind that wrote over any good times. Here in London, or at his other base in New York, he didn't have to remember.

He didn't have to face the past. It didn't have to shape who he was.

Then all that had changed with his father's illness. He'd been forced to return to Sicily. Forced back into his brother's life. The twin who'd destroyed Rafe's planned future as though it was nothing more than paper. The only two women he'd got close to had been lost. His mother and then Emma. Damn it, he'd lost Emma to his own brother. And now the final insult was that Rafe had no choice but to step up to the mark and do his duty, to help his father and his brother keep the Casella fortune.

Rafe pushed his troubles aside. This wasn't the time for them. Not when this woman was exactly what he needed right now. A distraction he wanted to lose himself in—completely.

'You didn't order champagne. You demanded it.' The stunned look on her face at being reprimanded made him smile. This was going to be a very entertaining evening. Precisely what he needed.

Tonight, he wanted to lose himself. Completely and with this woman. From the way she was looking at him, eyes swirling with desire as much as annoyance, he knew it was only a matter of time until he did just that. A sizzling sexual attraction drew them inexplicably to one another and he had no intention of severing it. Instead, he would meet it head-on.

'I did no such thing.'

'I didn't hear a please,' he taunted her, watching the gold flecks in her dark brown eyes shine brighter with fury. 'And I am yet to hear a thank you.'

Beneath her dark complexion he noticed she had the good grace to blush. She sighed, her breasts rising with the deep breath in, snagging his attention, ratcheting up his lust, tightening the binds of attraction.

Silence fell between them as the bartender poured two glasses of champagne, placing the bottle back in the cooler, before attending to other guests. She took hers and, still without a word of thanks, turned her attention away from him.

'Sorry. It's been a bad day,' she said quickly. 'A bad week. Two weeks, in fact.'

He watched her once more in the mirror as she sipped her drink, before putting the glass on the bar and tracing one long slender finger around the rim absently. Her thoughts far away from him. From this bar.

'That's both of us then.'

Her gaze met his in the mirror. They remained like that, gazes locked, drawing them together, keeping them linked. It was powerful. Hard to resist. But he had no intention of doing that. This beauty who'd exploded into his world was exactly the antidote he needed after this morning's meeting with his father.

'It might have just got a little better.' She tilted her head on one side, still watching him in the mirror. Again, the sparkle of diamonds hanging from her ears caught his attention as she openly flirted with him. Teased him.

Champagne. Diamonds. Who was this enigma of a woman who'd gate-crashed his private moment?

'Shall we agree to dismiss today? To live for now? This moment and nothing else?' He spoke to her reflection, not sure where his questions had come from.

He was the last person who would condone shirking duty for personal needs. But this woman's demeanour, her confident sexiness and charm, sparkling brighter than her diamonds, must be affecting him more than he knew.

She picked up her glass, raising it up to his reflection in the mirrors, her gaze intently holding his. In that hypnotic way a woman could seduce a man with just one look, he knew he was lost.

Tonight, he was hers.

'I will drink to that,' Kaliana said as she tried once again not to notice how incredibly sexy she found this man. Her friend and flatmate, Claire, had told her she needed to let go of the past. Get out there and have fun. Be the woman she really wanted to be.

So she'd thrown caution to the wind and headed out to do just that, planning to meet up with her friends as soon as they all finished work. But she'd never expected this. Not just the man himself, but an undeniable need to be with a man she didn't even know. And in a way she'd never experienced.

He was just the distraction she needed after today's call from her father, reminding her that two weeks had passed since she'd agreed to find a man wealthy enough to save her kingdom. And save herself from a marriage to a brutal bully.

Maybe Claire was right. Maybe she needed to find herself before she could find a husband. Had fate brought her this man for that exact reason? She focused on the stranger. His white shirt was open at the neck and, if she was brave enough to look lower, more than hinted at his bronzed and well-defined chest, dusted with dark hair.

That same call of hungry need which had first zipped through her when she'd looked at his handsome face, into his intensely black eyes, unfurled once more. It wasn't like her at all. She'd always avoided men like him. Dangerously sexy men. Men who could make her want the impossible. Men who could make her forget. Because she didn't want to forget Alif and their innocent young love.

But tonight she needed this. She had no intention of avoiding anything or anyone. She wanted to take whatever the evening offered. When she'd seen the handsome stranger, glaring into his drink, she'd known with an unnerving certainty that he was what she wanted. What she needed.

Tonight, she wanted to be a different woman. She wanted a distraction. She needed the rebellion against the hand fate had dealt her. That need burned brighter than ever. Pushing her on. Making her want to taste what could have been.

You want him. A voice echoed in her mind, chanting and triumphant. The little miss prim and proper virgin she'd always been wanted this sex god of a man. And why shouldn't she have some fun? Rebellion rippled through her again, stronger than ever. Nobody would ever know if she had a little bit of fun. Indulged in a bit of flirting. Not here in London. Not so far away from Ardu Safra. In London she was simply Kaliana. Nobody knew her here and she could hide from her weighty royal title.

Excitement zipped through her. Maybe it was time to taste even more than that. Maybe it was time to finally let go of the past, of who she'd been, and discover what physically being with a man was like. But not just any man. This man.

She looked up into the stranger's face to see a slow sexy smile spread across his lips. Heat infused her cheeks. She knew he couldn't possibly read her mind, but she wondered if he had. If he knew just how much she wanted him.

He picked up his glass and raised it to her. 'A toast. To this moment.'

Her tongue slicked over suddenly parched lips, her breath seeming harder to come by. Less natural. Her heart thumped. Her body heated. She liked the way he made her feel. Liked the sensation of freedom and power this surge of sexual chemistry between them gave her. Freedom she might never know again if she did her duty by her family and made a marriage to financially save the kingdom of Ardu Safra.

The thought of the man she'd be forced to marry if she didn't make a deal with a man of her choice almost squashed her bravado. No, she inwardly berated herself. She wouldn't think of Nassif now or of how her life would be if they married. All she wanted to think about was this moment. *This* man.

'To the moment,' she said boldly, hoping she didn't sound as gauche and inexperienced as she really was.

She'd never chatted up a man like this before. Never given out such a clear message of wanting far more than idle chat to any man other than the man she'd once been engaged to. Yet here she was. Alone. In a bar. With a sinfully sexy man. Not wanting the moment to end.

She sipped her champagne. All the while

his inky black eyes watched her, his brow slightly furrowed. His stubble-covered jaw was stern and set. He looked powerful. Commanding. And sexy.

He called to her on a level she'd never known existed. Made her want the impossible. Made her want to be someone else—for tonight at least. Something no other man had made her feel since Alif's death.

'Allow me to introduce myself,' he said, his gravelly voice sending spirals of heat through her, nudging at the need, the attraction he raised. Demanding the kind of satisfaction she knew instinctively only he could give her.

'Just first names,' she said quickly, watching his brows raise before a smile of conspiracy slid slowly over his lips. Sinfully sexy didn't come anywhere near it.

'As you wish.' He lifted his glass of champagne to her, his eyes darkening with wild desire, making her head spin more than the champagne she wasn't really used to. 'Rafe.'

'Ana,' she said quickly, unable to quell the shimmer of excitement rushing through her.

The feeling was so powerful she drank the

remainder of her champagne in one go, not missing his amusement, which set off sparks in his eyes as well as inside her. He pulled the bottle of champagne from the cooler, ice rattling as it was disturbed and, without a word, replenished her glass.

When he looked at her again his expression was speculative, but thankfully he didn't say anything, didn't ask further questions. Instead he replaced the bottle in the ice with the kind of familiarity that made her think he must be a waiter. Maybe he worked here? Maybe he'd just finished for the night?

'Are you a waiter here?' she asked as he took a sip of his champagne.

His eyes widened and for a moment she thought the champagne he'd sipped would be fired all over her. She'd clearly shocked him. Offended him even. She'd been so taken in by him she hadn't paid that much attention to his clothes—just him. But now she looked more closely, she could see his shirt wasn't just any shirt. It was quality, fitting him to perfection, and had probably been made for him.

'No. I am a guest. As are you, I presume.'

'I am,' she said with renewed determination. She knew that whatever happened next—and the fact that something would was as certain as the full moon which would rise over London—she wanted this night.

She was a woman with needs. A woman with desires. A woman this man had set alight with one sexy smile.

She was more than entitled to this one night. She'd lost the love of her life and soon she would be forced into a marriage she didn't want. This moment was hers. And she intended to take it. All of it.

'Then I am honoured to be able to share this evening with you.' He glanced at her, pouring himself another glass of champagne. She watched, mesmerised by his olive hands, long regal fingers, wrapping around the bottle so eloquently.

What would it feel like to have those hands touch her? To have those fingers bring pleasure to her body?

He looked directly at her, a mysterious intensity in his eyes as they slowly travelled down her body, lingering on her breasts, the soft silk of her pale gold blouse offering no protection against the heat of his eyes. His attention lowered, down over the skirt of the same silk, fitting snugly to her hips. Then finally, when Kaliana thought she couldn't take it any more, his attention shifted to her high-heeled sandals and red painted toenails.

She shivered with pleasure. Anticipation.

He hadn't touched her, but he'd just undressed her. Right here. In the bar of an exclusive hotel. She felt totally and gloriously naked even though the cool silk against her skin told her otherwise.

Did he know her thoughts? Did he know how he made her feel? Did he know what she wanted? Right now.

'I think all night would be better.' Emboldened by the heat of her body, she pushed aside embarrassment. Pushed aside the last remnants of her reservations and made her intentions, her needs, clear. Before she married to save her family from the shame of financial ruin, she wanted to know the pleasure of being desired by a man. The pleasure of desiring *this* man.

His brows flicked up in surprise but instantly he schooled his chiselled features, the cool charm of moments ago back in play. 'You wish to spend the entire night in my company?'

No man had ever come close to making her feel the kind of desire Alif had made her feel. If only she hadn't been so insistent on going to her marriage bed a virgin, she would have known what it was to desire and be desired before he'd been tragically taken from her. Regret rushed through her.

No other man had ever made her feel that way.

Until she'd seen this man. Within seconds of her eyes meeting his she'd known she wanted him. Known he was the only man who could cleanse her body of its innocence.

She wasn't about to allow this moment, this feeling, this need, to slip away again. She wanted this night. Wanted this man. 'I do.' She held his gaze, challenging him to pull back, to call a halt to the dangerous game of passion she was on the brink of playing. 'I want to be with you all night.'

Kaliana wanted to indulge in the game, dangerous or not. What better way to forget about the future and move on from the past than in this man's arms?

His gaze narrowed. Was he thinking of a wife he'd left at home? Children even? 'You are playing a dangerous game, Ana.'

The silky softness of his voice was like a caress. It soothed. It excited. If his voice could do that, what would his kiss be like?

Her gaze flew to his lips; instantly a slow and very sexy smile spread over them.

'A game I want to play.' She looked up at him from lowered lashes, flirting coming surprisingly naturally to her. 'But if you don't want to. Or can't...' She allowed the words to trail off, seductively moving closer to him in a way she'd never, ever imagined herself doing. But tonight she wasn't herself. She looked boldly up at him. 'I will go.'

Instantly he put one arm around her waist, slowly but very purposefully drawing her closer. All the while his eyes remained fixed on hers. She moved willingly towards him, her body alive with a sensation she'd never experienced before. The pressure of his hand, his arm holding her, burning her skin.

'We will play the game your way.' His eyes darkened as he drew her a fraction closer, the narrowing gap between their bodies alive with sparks. 'For now.'

'Good.' She smiled up at him, feeling out of her depth and very much in control all at the same time. She moved closer still, inhaling the exotic scent of his cologne, the tang of citrus blending with cedarwood pushing her on, taking her higher. This was exactly the game she wanted to play.

Tonight, she wasn't Princess Kaliana of Ardu Safra. Tonight, she was simply Ana and it felt right. Tonight, she wanted this man. He was exactly what she needed. What she wanted. And she wanted him all night.

CHAPTER TWO

RAFE WATCHED ANA'S eyes darken. Desire thundered through him. Harder. Faster. Like the call of a war drum of old. He was losing the mask of the composed businessman who'd a short while ago been drinking whisky alone. Hell, he was losing himself. And he hadn't even kissed her.

Yet.

With this woman's body pressed so alluringly against his, he knew he was in danger of completely losing his grasp on reality. Losing everything. His whole body ached for her and the satisfaction he knew only she could give. He'd never been so hard. So ready.

She moved closer, her smoky eyes filling with need, exploding with desire. Shimmying her hips provocatively, pressing against his erection. And he thought he'd never been so hard.

He tightened his hold on her, keeping her delicious body against him. 'See what you do to me?' He barely recognised the coarse rasp of his voice.

She smiled. Moved her hips again, forcing him to bite down hard on the growl of desire threatening to rip from him.

'I feel,' she purred. Damn, but she was a merciless tease. 'But I don't see.'

He couldn't hold back any longer. He had to taste her. Had to feel her lips beneath his. Feel the passion that burnt in her eyes, taste it on her tongue as it danced with his.

But if he gave into that need here?

It wasn't worth imagining. Or was it? Erotic images swept through his mind, faster than lightning. Their bodies entwined in the erotic dance of desire.

Rafe inhaled deeply as she pressed her body even harder against his. Making those images so hot they became X-rated.

'I think we should retire to my suite.' His voice was hoarse and ragged with desire. He hadn't known anything like it. Ever. It was like a wild fire bearing down on him at an alarming pace, offering no escape. Not that he wanted any escape.

There was a slight pause as she looked up at him. A hint of uncertainty and hesitation. The fire cooled briefly, stilled, as if waiting to see which way the wind would take it. As he watched her, she looked innocent. Vulnerable. Then it was gone. The sex siren, the seductress, was back in play and the fire raged on relentlessly.

'And I was enjoying this moment.' She raised her brows, looking up at him, bringing her lips tantalisingly close to his. 'I was enjoying my power over you.'

'If you carry on with this power game, I am going to have to kiss you. Right here. Right now.' His voice was more of a feral growl, the like of which he'd never heard before. How could one woman, a woman he'd only just met, have such an effect on him?

'Then kiss me. Right here and right now.' Her bold and brazen reply excited him further. There would be no backing out now. This would be taken to the inevitable conclusion—in the privacy of his suite.

She moved closer still, her breath feathering his lips. 'Kiss me.'

Hell, he couldn't wait any longer. He had to taste her. She moved her lips closer, a spark of sexy mischief in her eyes. He placed his champagne glass on the bar, not taking his eyes from hers, and spread his palm over her shoulder blades, at the same time crushing her lips beneath his.

She gasped into his mouth, her eyes wide, and again that aura of innocence briefly shone through. A woman playing with fire. The fire of desire. Desire he could no longer control. She closed her eyes, long lashes sweeping down over her cheeks as she began to kiss him back. As hard and demanding as his kiss, sweeping away any doubts.

This woman was far from innocent. This was a woman in control of her sexuality. A woman who knew exactly what she wanted. And right now he was in no doubt. She wanted him.

Her tongue entwined with his and her arms wound round his neck, her fingers sliding into his hair, long nails scratching his scalp.

He delved his tongue deeper into her mouth, tasting champagne. Tasting her.

He had to get them out of here. He was in danger of ripping her sexy tight blouse and skirt from her body right here in the bar.

He lifted his lips away from hers reluctantly, dragging in a deep breath of sanity.

'Your suite,' she whispered, opening her eyes and looking up at him. Already she looked deliciously tousled.

Lust pounded through him. He barely had any control left. Virtually no restraint. His need for this woman, this moment, was so intense. He wanted to revel in her power. Be tamed by her. It either stopped here and now or…

'This is what you want?' He tried to steady his voice, needing to calm the heated desire thundering through him like a sudden eruption from Mount Etna. Despite this desire, despite the way her body begged him for more than just a kiss, he needed to hear her say it.

Did he really have to ask?

'It is,' Kaliana said softly, her voice husky,

her breathing rapid and uneven. He was giving her the chance to back out, proving he wanted her as much as she wanted him. Giving her the power. Power which made her feel alive.

She brushed her lips over his lightly, wanting to kiss away the control he'd suddenly found. She wanted him at her mercy. Her at his. She breathed against his lips, driven by a need too powerful to resist. 'It is. Take me to your suite.'

He held her gaze, looking deep into her eyes, as if satisfying himself she spoke the truth and for a moment she wondered if he knew. If he'd guessed she was a virgin. As if he'd guessed her act of bold bravado was exactly that. Was this man of undeniable experience about to turn her down? Leaving her aching for him, for satisfaction? Leaving her not knowing what it would be like to be sexually fulfilled?

She wanted this night of pleasure, this night of unknown desires. She needed it. To prove she was alive. Locked within her was the woman Alif had gently coaxed into the first flush of womanhood with his love.

She held her breath.

Pain rushed through her at the thought of Alif and the love they'd shared. The passion they should have known together. Was it wrong she felt such desire with another man?

She looked up at Rafe, felt the pull of attraction, the spark of desire, the heat of passion. It wasn't wrong. Something this powerful couldn't be. Unexpected, but not wrong.

'I want you,' she whispered, drawing again on the elation of being free to indulge in this desire. Free to be a woman who knew what she wanted and took it.

And she wanted this night and this man. Nobody except Rafe could stop it now. Tonight, she would finally bloom into the woman she could be.

'And I want you.' His accent suddenly deepened, the intensity in those dark eyes mirroring every need and emotion inside her.

'I want you to make love to me.' Her breath was ragged, her words slipping out, firm and decisive. Elation at her freedom, her power of abandonment to be exactly what she wanted, rose ever higher. She wanted to feel his kisses all over her body. His strong hands caressing her, pleasuring her in ways she could only imagine. For too long she'd locked herself behind a barrier of grief, but she couldn't do it any more. Not if she had to give up on everything she'd ever dared to hope for and sacrifice her secret dreams of one day finding the kind of love she'd shared with Alif. If love a second time even existed. 'I want you to make love to me. Tonight.'

'Tonight?' The hoarseness of his voice left her in no doubt he was fighting a losing battle as much as she was.

'Tonight,' she teased. 'All night.'

He inhaled deeply, his eyes piercing into hers. Taking her hand, he silently led her through the serene calmness of the hotel bar, some guests casting them curious but knowing glances.

Together they stepped into the lift. The air crackled with tension. Neither moved. Towards each other or away. The only contact was her hand in his. Silence enveloped them as the lift moved swiftly upwards. She didn't dare look at him. Something wild was about to explode between them and if they even so much as looked at one another it would happen before they reached the privacy of his suite.

She drew in a deep breath, his scent stirring her desire ever higher, and she willed the lift to stop. Willed the doors to open. Beside her, he was rigid, his body motionless with control as he stared straight ahead. She didn't need to look at him to know it. She sensed it. Sensed the power of his control.

At last the lift doors swished almost silently open, directly into his suite, so vast she was sure it must occupy the entire floor. So, he was immensely wealthy. Not the waiter she'd mistaken him to be.

She smiled at the memory of his reaction to her question as she walked into the suite, past the sprawling pale grey sofa, covered with cushions. Past the vast desk where papers and a closed laptop confirmed he was a businessman. Towards the wall of windows which looked out over London, now twinkling with many lights, competing with the moon.

She closed her eyes, inhaling deeply. Here, tonight, she could be a different woman than the one who'd handed over her future to the family duty she'd always secretly hoped to be free of, wishing instead for love and happiness. Here, tonight, none of that mattered.

Awareness prickled over her skin as he came to stand behind her, his hands gently holding her upper arms, subtly caressing them, pulling her slowly closer to him.

She looked at the window, their reflection, just as erotic as it had been in the bar. She watched him lower his head to kiss her neck, anticipating his lips on her skin seconds before it happened. She closed her eyes to the pleasure, her pulse racing wildly.

She sighed softly as his lips trailed over her skin, burning it. Setting her alight. But it wasn't enough. Nowhere near enough.

Kaliana angled her head, inviting more, needing more. She leant her head back against him as he drew her closer. Rafe's fingertips joined the torture his lips were inflicting on her skin. She shuddered with pleasure as the warmth of his fingers traced downwards, inside her blouse. Inside her bra.

She pressed her eyes tightly shut, desire wildly uncoiling deep inside her. Deep in the hidden femininity she'd locked away after losing Alif.

Rafe murmured against her neck, his fingers grazing over her increasingly hard nipples. It was exquisite. She trembled with need as he continued his torture, heated desire burning between her legs. She sighed softly as she turned her head to face him. He moved closer, the torture on her nipple continuing as he slicked his tongue over her lips. He moved slowly back and she licked her lips, tasting champagne and whisky along with something stronger. Desire.

He slid his hand away from her breast, trailing a blaze of heat up her neck. Every part of her was on high alert. Every part of her wanted him. Needed him.

She turned in his arms, clutched at his shirt and pulled, wanting to feel his body, needing to see it. Buttons popped to the floor as she dragged the shirt out from his black trousers, pushing it aside, pressing her lips to his bare chest. Tasting him. Inhaling his powerful masculinity.

She had no idea where the wanton woman she'd become had come from, but he tasted so good. His skin felt delicious on her tongue. He held the tops of her arms tightly as he spoke in another language and somewhere in the back of her mind she knew it was Italian. Then the carnal heat of desire took over, consuming her as it exploded into life.

'See what you do to me.' He spoke English with a harsh whisper. Had she imagined his words in Italian?

'No,' she said, spreading her palms on his chest. Pushing them through the silky soft hair that covered his well-defined chest muscles, smiling at the game she was playing once more with him. 'No, I don't see. Not at all.'

He laughed, a soft sexy laugh, unwinding the coil of desire inside her even more. 'Maybe I should remove my clothes?'

She smiled, heat and power rampaging

through her, making her bolder and braver than ever. There was no way she could stop now. 'Maybe you should.'

'In that case, my sweet, sexy nymph...' He took his arms from around her, pulling off his shirt and stepping back a pace. He tossed the ruined shirt aside, his eyes never leaving hers, the hungry sparks of passion in them making her breathless. She looked at his chest, his shoulders, his strong arms, her attention lingering on a tattoo on his upper right arm.

The Italian words, *Vivi con passione*, inked on his skin fired through her, making this moment more intense. *Live with passion—* that was exactly what she intended to do. Tonight. With this man.

'I still don't see,' she teased him further, determined not to be side-tracked by the bold dark words inked against his beautiful olive skin.

With a wicked smile he slowly, deliberately and very tantalisingly removed the remainder of his clothes. His body toned and perfect. His erection large and proud. 'Now do you see?'

She should be shocked, embarrassed even. But she wasn't. How could she be when this was precisely what she wanted? To see him in all his masculine glory. To revel in the power she had over his body—over him.

She didn't answer his question but began to roughly pull at her blouse, desperate to take off every last barrier between them. To be as free as he was. Liberated from her lifelong prison as Princess of the ancient kingdom of Ardu Safra. Even if it was only for one night.

'Allow me, *cara*.' He moved back towards her, reaching out with steady hands to unfasten her blouse, button by button. Then he pushed the silk off her shoulders and it slithered to the floor as he unfastened the belt of her skirt before reaching behind her to the zip fastening. The action brought him close, so very close. She was painfully aware of his naked, aroused body, but he didn't touch her—only her clothes.

He pulled the zip of the skirt lower until the pale gold fabric slithered down over her hips, watching her as she stepped out of it and towards him. His gaze raked down over her skimpy bra and panties, down her legs to her gold heels. She wanted to be as naked as him. Be his equal.

Without taking her eyes from him she slipped off first one sandal, kicking it aside. Then the other. The thud it made on the floor almost as loud as her pounding heart. Reaching behind her, she unclasped her bra, acutely aware of his eyes devouring her, waiting. She let the bra fall to the floor.

She lowered her hands to her panties, her gaze still fixed on his, unable to believe the wild desire she saw burning in them.

'No,' he said, his hand covering hers. He was so close she could feel the heat coming off him. Feel the need in his body for her.

'No?' she questioned.

'No.' Rafe looked into Ana's eyes, the thud of desire so loud in his veins, surely the whole of London must hear it. 'Not yet.'

She moved closer, reaching up, pressing her lips against his, her breasts brushing his chest. His control snapped and in one swift move he wrapped her in his embrace, claiming her lips in a hungry kiss. Her hungry need matching his. Demand for demand. Passion for passion. Their breathing hard and loud as desire threatened to totally consume them.

He needed to slow things down. Needed to take this night of unexpected pleasure more slowly. It would be the last he ever had because, even though his bride would be one brokered in a boardroom, he would remain faithful. He would never know a night like this again. Never know this carnal need for a woman after he was married.

He pushed those dark thoughts from his mind. They were for tomorrow. This almost naked, sexy vision of desire was tonight.

Her hand slid down his chest as she moved her body slightly away from his. Instinctively he tensed as her touch slid over his abs, then lower. Her palm pressed against him, then her fingers wrapped around him, exploring him.

The thought excited him more. Making him harder.

'So beautiful,' she whispered, looking down, as if she'd never seen a naked man before. She moved her hand upwards, then down and he bit back a groan of passionate despair. He had to stop her. Had to regain control. He wanted to pleasure her before she literally brought him to his knees at the altar of desire.

'Now you have seen—and felt,' he said, taking her hand in his. 'It's my turn.'

Her eyes widened a little and a faint blush spread over her cheeks, but desire pushed him on and, lowering his head, he took one hardened nipple in his mouth.

She gasped, her fingers delving into his hair as he slicked his tongue around her nipple, enjoying the shudder of pleasure which ran over her again and again. Then he stood up, pressing himself to her, feeling the heat of her body, her naked pert breasts against his chest. He kissed her—until she clung to him, her body begging his for release.

The loss of control threatened him again and he lowered his head, smiling as her fingers pushed into his hair, gently guiding him to where she wanted to be kissed next. He obliged, lavishing the same attention on her other breast.

'Don't stop,' she gasped, and satisfaction

rushed through him. The little spitfire who'd walked into the bar demanding champagne had been tamed by desire. But he wasn't done with her yet. Nowhere near it. He wanted her to cry out with passion.

He murmured soft words of Italian as he kissed down her stomach, pressing his lips against the lacy cream panties, feeling her body arch towards him.

In one effortless move he pulled the lace down to her ankles, returning to the intimate dark hair. Holding her buttocks, he knelt before her, kissing into the silky soft hair. She placed her hands on his head, parting her legs slightly. He looked up at her and moved one hand to caress the soft skin inside her thigh, before trailing his finger intimately over her.

He stifled a groan of pleasure as he felt her eagerness, lust firing through him. Lust he had to ignore. He wanted to pleasure her, make this moment last.

'I never knew,' she gasped as he leaned forward and tasted her.

Never knew what? His question came and

went, obliterated by a need to really taste her. To totally and completely possess her.

'Oh,' she cried out as waves of ecstasy racked her body, leaving her gasping, clinging to him as he continued his torment.

Instead of calming his need, giving him more control, hearing her cries of pleasure with such abandon only increased it. He wanted to be inside her. Deep inside her.

Kaliana shuddered as the intense pleasure of her first orgasm subsided. She'd been so lost in it, so swept away in delirium that only now was she aware he'd stood up, taken her hand and was drawing her towards the sofa.

He sat down, and she watched in fascination as he rolled on the condom he must have had in readiness for this moment.

The moment she gave herself to him.

Should she tell him she'd never had sex before? That he was the first man who had brought her to such a shuddering orgasm? Would he even know after what he'd just done to her?

He leant forward, taking her hand, drawing her closer. 'Come here.'

Before she had time to wonder where she should go, how she should sit with him, he pulled her onto his lap, her legs astride his. She was completely out of her depth, but it was wild and reckless and right now exactly what she needed. What she wanted.

'You are so beautiful,' he said softly, his eyes swirling with desire as his hand slid between her legs, touching her where, after her orgasm, she felt sensitive, so in need of more. He leant forward, taking her nipple in his mouth while his fingers slid into her.

It was too much. Too nice. Surely, he couldn't take her to that dizzy place of oblivion again? So soon?

She lifted herself up, his torturous touch stopping as his hands moved to grasp her buttocks, his mouth leaving her nipple as he looked up at her.

'Cara mia.' He spoke quietly, his tone firm and commanding, the Italian words so enticing, so sexy. Confidence filled her, pushing her on in her quest to find herself, to discover just who she really was.

She dragged in a shuddering breath as his expert touch took her higher. It was so much more than she'd ever anticipated. So powerful. So... Words failed her. She was close to the edge again. Close to being lost in pleasure. She closed her eyes, her head falling forwards, her hair cascading around her, shielding her from the scrutiny of those dark eyes as she enjoyed the moment.

'Look at me, *cara,*' he demanded, more firmly this time.

Fighting the waves of passion and lifting her head, she looked at him. His eyes were dark and glittering like diamonds. Had he guessed she was a virgin? Did the ease with which he could push her to another orgasm give away her inexperience? Her innocence?

'I want to see you.' His voice was husky and incredibly sexy. 'I want to watch your face as you take me inside you.'

She drew in a breath at his boldness, shocked by how wild and wanton it made her. She wanted to feel him inside her. Deep inside her. It all seemed so right. How could she not want this man to possess her in the most intimate way?

Her gaze locked with his. She lifted her hips, lifted herself over him, hoping her boldness, her attempt to control, to dominate, would hide the nerves she couldn't help but feel. No matter how much she wanted this.

His fingers bit into her buttocks as he encouraged her to move lower. The tip of his heated hardness forced instinct to take over and she moved slowly. With her arms around him, she moved her body up then lowered herself back to him, controlling the moment. Teasing him. Tormenting herself. Each movement making her bolder.

He gripped her buttocks tighter as she lowered herself again, a feral growl coming from him as he lifted himself up, sliding into her in one hard move. She cried out as a burning pain snatched her from the moment. He stilled. Deep inside her, he didn't move. Those dark eyes were full of questions. Full of doubt.

She didn't want that. Not now. Not until

they'd both lost themselves in the oblivion of passion. She wanted that abandonment. Needed it. She wanted that ultimate climax to this moment. Questions could wait. Everything could wait.

She forced herself to move, lifting herself up, then lowering herself again, stoking the desire back up. He watched her intently as she controlled the moment. Controlled him.

His desire returned instantly. She could see it in his eyes. Feel it inside her as she continued to move up and down. The sensation of having him inside her was so much more intense than she'd anticipated. She continued to move until he swore savagely as he lost control, as he gave into what her body wanted and began moving with her. Each movement faster and more furious than the last. Each movement pushing her ever closer to the edge.

'Mia bella!' he cried out, his release coming fast, dragging her with him into oblivion.

Her body shook with pleasure as she found her release, her total fulfilment. Her moment of complete abandon. Waves of ecstasy held her in their grip, tossing her in the sea of passion until she was sure she would drown.

Rafe's breathing calmed, his racing heart eased. Ana's body limply clung to his and he tried to make sense of what had just happened.

He'd taken her virginity. A gift so precious it should never have been his to take. He didn't deserve that. He couldn't give a woman like this any more than tonight, even if he wanted to. He looked at her—head bent, hair cascading around her face, hiding her from him, from his scrutiny. His questions. Those moments of hesitation in the bar, that aura of innocence, had been real. That woman had been a virgin—until she'd accompanied him to his suite.

She lifted her head, still sitting astride him, looking down at him anxiously. He saw it then so clearly. The confidence of her actions earlier had deceived him. Her bravado. Her wild wantonness. Her complete power of seduction. It had all been an act. Had that innocence been there all along in her eyes?

Had he been so blinded by desire he hadn't seen it or—worse—ignored it?

He should have seen it. Should have stopped. Should have been in control. But what they'd just shared, from the very moment she'd first looked at him, had been unlike anything he'd ever known.

'You should have told me.' His voice was firm, steady and steely controlled. Which, considering a very naked woman still sat astride his lap, was no mean feat.

'Losing my virginity to you—tonight—was my decision to make.' The bold, confident woman who'd walked into the bar earlier and demanded champagne was back.

She agilely moved herself away from him and stood up, proudly naked in front of him as if to prove her point. Daring him to deny her claim. She was right. Of course she was right. Yet he couldn't shake the nagging sensation that he'd taken something he shouldn't have.

'It was also my decision to take it—or not.' He reached forward, snatching up his hastily discarded trousers, pulling them on.

How the hell had this happened? He'd

claimed this alluring woman's virginity in an unplanned night of passion when he'd just relented, just accepted that marriage, purely for convenience, was something he had to do.

He looked at her. Would she now cling to him? Cling to this moment, believing there was something more between them? Something he couldn't ever give any woman.

'You can rest assured that I have no intention of demanding anything other than tonight from you. I am not looking for long-term commitment and I certainly don't crave the elusive happy-ever-after of marriage. Not from you. Not from any man.'

She stood defiantly before him, dark hair loose and wild about her shoulders, gloriously naked. The first fresh stirrings of desire began to wind themselves through his body. He fought to ignore that primal call. This night of uncomplicated sex had suddenly become as complicated as his life.

'Why tonight? Why me?' he asked, needing to know more, even though it would be a mistake. A mistake because that would make him think of her after tonight.

She looked at him, an air of defiance in her gaze. 'Five years ago I was engaged—to a man I loved. A man I wanted to marry—as a virgin.'

Rafe frowned as he digested this piece of information. 'What happened?' As the question found voice, he instinctively knew that, whatever had happened, it was more than a falling-out-of-love issue.

Ana bit her lower lip, the first sign of nervousness he'd seen her display. Something inside him shifted.

'One month before the wedding, he was killed in an accident.'

The mood in the room changed, the tension increasing. 'I'm sorry.'

She moved closer to him, reminding him, if he needed it, that she was naked. 'What is your story?'

Her question took him off guard, his mind partly occupied by her admission and partly by the slow burn of desire striking up once more.

'My story?' He didn't want to do this. Didn't

want to spoil the passion of all they'd just shared with emotional issues.

'Why tonight and why me?' she said, echoing his question.

He laughed, desperate to calm the tension building higher than the desire of moments ago. 'When a beautiful woman crosses my path, I'm not going to walk the other way.'

She looked hurt by his humour, his attempt to derail the conversation. His attempt to keep his secrets safe. Hell, she'd been honest with him, shared her pain, even if only briefly. It wasn't as if they were in a relationship. They'd never see one another again. Didn't he owe it to her?

Guilt forced his words out. 'I have to get married.'

The room suddenly filled with a heavy silence as Ana looked at him, her eyes narrowing slightly in disbelief.

'Have to?' Then her frown disappeared as she drew her own conclusion. 'You are going to be a father?'

'No, not that.' Rafe sighed. 'Although that would be a lot less complicated.'

Ana hugged her arms around herself, looking chilled. He turned to pick up his discarded shirt, then placed it gently over her shoulders, his hands lingering longingly. She looked too sexy in his shirt.

'I don't understand.' She turned to look up at him. Her expression, so serious, as if it really mattered to her. As if she understood.

'My brother, Enzo, and I are twins. Our family has much wealth and property to hand onto the next generation. My father is terminally ill, and my brother has chosen this moment to inform him that he is unable to father a child, that his marriage is in trouble because of it. My father cannot see past the fact that the family name will not continue unless I marry and have a son.'

He'd never talked so openly, always guarded himself, but Ana had set something free within him. Frustration. It tore through him. Frustration for all he must do and because this moment was lost to such a discussion. Annoyance that the duty he had to prepare to undertake could snatch away even this night from him.

He looked down into Ana's eyes, the gold flecks in them so bright, so full of desire that it took his breath away. 'No more talking,' she whispered, reaching up to kiss him.

'No more talking,' he said huskily, desire pounding through him once more. He wanted her again. Right now.

'Then what are we going to do?' she teased, as if sensing his need to change the subject, to revive the passion between them.

She giggled seductively as he scooped her up, carrying her across the apartment to the bedroom. He felt free. Alive. And it couldn't end. Not yet.

'Make love all night.' He lowered her onto his bed before covering her body with his. 'That is what you want, isn't it?'

'So very much,' she said as she kissed him, setting fire to the embers of desire again. Whatever this was between them, it was far from over.

CHAPTER THREE

August—Palermo, Sicily

'THIS EVENING IS going to be a great success. Pure Seas and Oceans is really getting noticed now,' the coordinator of events informed Rafe as he scanned his speech for the final time. 'We even have someone from Charity Resources' London headquarters in attendance.'

'Really? How did you pull that one off?' Rafe asked, intrigued enough to look up.

'I have been working with Kaliana for the last month on this event, so when she said she wanted to attend tonight, how could I say no?' The triumphant look on the young man's face made Rafe smile. 'And she's requested a meeting with you afterwards.'

'Then who am I to disappoint someone who has helped our cause? After all, the charity needs all the exposure and promotion it can get.' Cleaning up the seas around the globe was something Rafe was as passionate about as he was his own renewable energy business. He'd agreed to be patron of the charity, hoping to help the cause. Judging by the expected turnout for this evening's event, having Charity Resources behind them must be having a good impact. The whole evening looked as though it would far exceed his expectations.

All the preparation for tonight had been better than dwelling on the ever-pressing need for him to find a wife. His father's health was not good and now Enzo had taken on the role of protector of their family's future. He'd even had the audacity to call Rafe and remind him time was not on their side, pushing him towards marriage, worried about the family fortune. Where was Enzo's remorse for all he'd done? Rafe had long ago let go of his love for Emma, but this threatened to permanently destroy the tense relationship between him and his twin for good.

His father's diagnosis made that family duty impossible to ignore. The noose around

Rafe's neck was tightening. He didn't want marriage. Or a family. How could Enzo do this and expect him to step in where he had failed?

Rafe shook his head in annoyance. He was allowing his problems to infiltrate his commitments. He wasn't here to find a way out of this situation; instead, he had to keep his focus where it needed to be. Once this event was over, then he would give serious consideration to just how he was going to find a woman to marry—without bringing emotion and sentiment into it. He needed a marriage deal.

Annoyed with himself for letting those thoughts in now, he left the hall as the guests began to arrive and headed backstage. Rafe needed to try and shake off the anger induced by just thinking about Enzo and what he'd done.

Instead, he allowed his mind to drift back to that night in London. To the one and only time he'd ever had a real connection with a woman. Something that might have gone beyond pure sexual attraction had she not run out on him, slipping from his bed in the early hours while he'd slept.

He pushed that memory away, refusing to care. Refusing to be affected by the emotional intimacy he and Ana had shared so briefly that night. Refusing to think what could have come of that night if he didn't have duty hanging over him. If he and Ana had taken longer to explore that powerful sexual chemistry between them.

Emotions threatened to cascade over him—emotions he would never allow. Still the image of Ana wouldn't leave his mind. Why hadn't he found out who she really was? Two months on, she still had a hold on his imagination. His body. Why did he crave her still?

He'd tried to tell himself it was for the best, that she'd left without asking for more than just that night, without even leaving her full name or number. But it had jarred his ego. She'd had her fill of him, but he had been left wanting more. Not a situation he was used to at all.

Rafe shut his mind to those thoughts. Tonight was important. He had to make an impact on the audience, the many influential businessmen and women who could help. And especially the visitor from Charity Resources. If she wanted a private meeting with him, he was going to ensure he got her backing for the cause.

The spotlight was well and truly on Rafe as he made his speech. He kept his focus on several influential business owners in the audience but he could feel intense scrutiny from the front row. From where the visitor from Charity Resources had been assigned a seat. The lighting was too bright, he couldn't see the faces of anyone in the front row and it wasn't until he'd finished and the audience applauded that the lights burning on him dimmed. Finally, he could see who had been watching his every move for the last half an hour.

His breath turned to fire in his lungs. His heartbeat thudded to a halt.

It was her.

Ana.

The hot, sexy siren who'd filled his dreams since that night in London sat in the front row where the visitor from Charity Resources should be sitting. The slim-fitting black dress offset with a pearl necklace couldn't disguise her. There was no mistake. It was Ana. His body kick-started into life again, his heart thumping, his breath shallow and rapid.

Ana. Or, as he'd been informed, Kaliana. His mystery woman of passion. The woman who'd given him her virginity, creating a connection between them he hadn't been able to sever. He bit back the harsh obscenity, wishing he'd kept himself up-to-date with the event's organisation while he'd been away from Sicily. But that was what he paid his event organiser for.

Shock mixed with the heady, heated need flowing in his veins. Unbidden, the spirited beauty of that night in London flashed into his mind, overriding the elegant vision who sat in the front row.

He saw the woman of that night again, her naked body so perfectly formed. He felt the telltale scorch of the heat of desire which had erupted in him like the volcano of his homeland.

Enough. He gritted his teeth against the slow slug of lust which echoed in his body, his limbs, his mind, even now. The persistent and unsatisfied ache of need. The annoyance that she'd walked away, keeping his lust very much alive.

The air in the room became heavy as those gold-flecked dark eyes met his, alive with sparks of mischief and laughter. Did she think this was amusing? He couldn't look away. All he wanted to do was drink in this vision. Savour the sexy body that had filled his restless nights all too often.

She smiled, cracking the veneer of control she wore so well. *Dio mio*, why had fate seen fit to tempt him once again with this woman?

The audience began to leave, chatting among themselves as they went. Rafe made his way towards the woman who'd got completely under his skin. A woman he'd never expected to see again. The woman, damn it—who'd given him her virginity then walked out of his life as if it was nothing.

The sensation of being a stallion at stud reared up again. But wasn't that exactly what his father wanted him to be? Needed him to be?

Ana moved to him and offered her hand. By some miracle Rafe maintained his composure. 'Ana,' he said, his voice harder than he'd heard it for a long time. 'Or is it Kaliana?' What kind of fool had he been to allow himself to be so utterly seduced by her charm? Her sexiness.

No questions.

The voice of reproach careered around in his head. But *she* had seduced him then left without a word. Why? Questions raged through him as he looked at her. The expression on her face was calm and devoid of emotion. Was it possible he had been fooled? That she hadn't just happened to be in the bar that night and found him irresistible. But, instead, had she set out to seduce him—and he had willingly allowed it to happen? Why had he believed her story about the loss of her fiancé?

Because you wanted her. At any price.

Her brows rose in haughty indignation. Was that amusement dancing in the gold flecks of her eyes, behind the superiority which radiated off her in waves? 'Is there somewhere we can talk privately?'

The audacity of the woman. To boldly stand before him, so regal and elegant on the surface, while he knew, with every nerve cell in his body, the sex siren he'd first met simmered beneath her refined exterior.

'Talk?' Talking was not something she'd been much interested in last time.

'I have a proposition to put to you.' The firmness of her voice couldn't quite disguise the huskiness and he couldn't resist the urge to tease her.

'I think, *Ana...*' he deliberately used the name she'd given him that night, satisfied when her cheeks flushed '...that you may have already done that.'

Annoyance sparked in her eyes. 'I have a deal to put to you. A business deal that will be of benefit to both of us.'

Rafe laughed softly as she glared up at him. She was challenging him, not just with her words, her request, but with her body. Yes, that sex siren was still there—and fighting for release.

'A deal?'

'Yes, a deal.' Her voice was sharp as she looked around her, suddenly seeming uncertain. Nervous. 'Is there somewhere private we can talk?'

What was she doing? Why had she thought this was a good idea? That it would work?

Kaliana followed Rafe into the small office and waited until the door had closed tightly behind them. She didn't want anyone else to be a witness to what she had to say to Raffaele Casella, the man she'd given herself to with complete abandon.

Ever since that night she had dreamed of seeing him again. Dreamed that he would find her and tell her that night had been more than just passion. More than just lust. That he would tell her he loved her. Each one a fanciful dream which had faded once the light of day dispelled the magic.

That night she'd glimpsed the possibility that love could happen for her again. That out there, somewhere, was a man who could make her happy again. A man who could love her as much as Alif had. Ever since that realisation she'd been torn apart by guilt. Did the fact that she yearned for love make what she and Alif had shared any less real?

Never in her wildest dreams had she thought she would see Rafe again—or that she would be seeking him out so boldly. She could still hear Claire's advice now as her friend had made one last-ditch attempt to stop her.

'So what if he is the man who gave you the most pleasurable night of your life? You can't go to Sicily and ask him to marry you.' Panic had been in every word Claire had spoken, as well as in her expression.

'He is wealthy. He needs to not only marry, but to have a son. He is everything I need to escape marriage to Nassif.'

'But marriage, Kal,' Claire had pleaded.

But Kaliana had no choice. Not any more. It was barely two months until her twenty-sixth birthday—and her wedding day. There was no way the man waiting for her at the altar was going to be Nassif. No way at all. Even Claire understood that.

'And how may I assist you?' There was an aloofness in Rafe's voice as he looked at her, his back to the door, his face as impassive as stone. He hadn't looked at her like that the last time she'd seen him. Then his eyes had burned with passion, sparked with wild desire. For her.

She gathered her composure. Fought the urge to turn and leave. To run. But she couldn't. She needed a husband. And she'd made her choice. 'I have a deal to put to you, Signor Casella. One that will be of benefit to both of us.'

His brows flicked up. 'I'm sure we can dispense with such formalities, Ana. I'd much prefer Rafe.' This time his voice held a hint of the man she'd met in London. A hint of the man who'd shown her what real passion could be like.

She relaxed a little. 'And I'd prefer Kaliana.'

'So, Kaliana, how can we benefit one another?' He walked towards her and the air seemed to have been sucked from the small office. Her heart was thudding as her body betrayed her, reacting to his nearness as if the last two months hadn't elapsed. As if only hours had passed since he'd taken her on such a wondrous journey of discovery. To a place where she'd discovered the sensual woman deep within her.

She pushed that image, that memory aside. The man before her now was different. Detached. Was it possible the man she'd given herself to in London was just part of her imagination, her wishful thinking? That her memory was tricking her? Did he even exist?

'In London, you told me you needed to marry.' She forced the words out over a tongue so dry it was almost impossible to sound in control, in charge.

Rafe stiffened, his expression impassive. Emotionless. She'd touched a nerve. A raw one. 'That is what I said, yes.'

This was harder than she'd imagined. His scrutiny, those dark piercing eyes, made her nervous. She swallowed down her nerves and gathered herself. Pushed on, before her courage failed her.

He narrowed his eyes suspiciously, watching her steadily, the tension in the room—in her body—increasing. 'What is this deal, exactly?'

'You also said that providing the next generation of your family fell to you.' Her words sounded calm. Cool and collected. Yet her heart was thumping. She clenched her hands, digging her red painted nails into her palms.

She could still feel the shock when she'd seen the photo of the patron of Pure Seas and Oceans while researching her new client. The image of the man she'd lost her virginity to in London smiling back at her. Not at all the waiter she'd first mistaken him for—or even the everyday businessman she'd later decided he was—but a man whose family and personal wealth was astounding.

A man who needed a wife and a son to continue the family name.

She'd stared at the image, her mind resisting the urge to revisit memories of that night as the realisation sank in that he could be the man to solve her problems, while she solved his. A mutually beneficial marriage arrangement. A marriage that could offer more still—the desire and intimacy her heart craved—if she was brave enough.

It had all seemed so simple. So clear-cut and easy to follow through on. Even on the flight here, it had seemed that way. But everything had changed as she'd sat watching him talk so passionately. He hadn't recognised her, even though she'd sat in the front row. Doubt had filed in.

Then he'd looked at her, his dark eyes locking with hers. He *had* recognised her.

Now, standing before his intense scrutiny, what she'd come here for was anything but simple.

'I understood you were here to represent Charity Resources. What does my personal life have to do with tonight's event?' There was a coldness in his voice. She could see his mind working, see the questions, the deep suspicion and mistrust flashing across his handsome face. A face she'd kissed. A face she'd pressed hers against as her body had been taken over by the pleasure of an orgasm.

'I know how it feels...' she paused, wishing she'd kept to her rehearsed script '...to be forced to marry.'

He frowned. 'I find that very hard to believe.'

She braced herself. If he didn't believe her, didn't feel something for her plight then she'd lost. She'd have to marry Nassif. 'It's true. My father is insisting I marry. He has even selected a husband.'

'That sounds like something from a movie, or a fairy tale.' He smiled at her and her heart flipped over as he moved closer, the atmosphere in the room changing instantly. Heating up. As if it were still that night. 'And are you going to marry this man?'

'No. I will do anything to avoid that.' Her response was instant. Full of indignation.

Rafe laughed again, his lips staying in a sexy smile, reminding her of their night together. 'So, Ana... Kaliana...have you come to share some kind of plan with me? One I can also use to find a wife?'

She smiled bravely at him, crossing her fingers. 'Actually, that is exactly what I am here for.'

He came so close to her that she could reach up and brush her lips over his. 'Then tell me, sweet Ana. What is this plan of yours?'

His eyes searched hers, dragging her mind and body back to the passion they'd shared. She couldn't think of that now. She had to remain focused. Had to put her deal to him in a strong and confident way. She had to be the Princess she was, not the woman he'd awakened. 'I will be your wife.'

'My wife?' He stepped back, his dark eyes thunderous as he looked at her, taking in every detail, scanning down over her body with suspicion. 'Are you pregnant?'

'No.' The response was instant, but she was ready for it. Claire had warned her he might think that and Kaliana sent up a silent prayer of thanks for her friend. For having at least one person on her side, willing to fight her battles with her. 'No, I'm not pregnant.'

'Then what the hell? *Dio mio*, Ana. Marriage!' He flung his hands up in a wild gesture of disbelief, his use of her name snagging at the remorse she'd felt walking out on him that morning. But her need to flee had been driven by guilt. Guilt that she'd enjoyed such a night with him. Sadness that she'd never known it with Alif, the man she'd loved. She'd been so torn she'd had to leave. Had to walk away whilst he slept.

'We both need to marry. Wouldn't it be better to marry one another than marry strangers?' She held her breath as he looked at her then walked past her, across the room to the window. He looked out at the view of Sicily's rugged coastline. She stood still, rooted to the spot. 'Or to accept partners arranged by our families?'

Rafe's silence did little to instil any kind of hope in her. The tension in the room was explosive as she watched him. His broad shoulders were rigid and square. He couldn't even look at her.

'Why do you need to marry, Ana?' He paused, continuing to glare out of the window, and for a moment she floundered, unable to find an answer. At least one that wouldn't give away just how much she'd wanted him. Wanted that night. Needed it. To know she was desirable for herself, not her title.

She sighed. She owed him this truth at least. 'I am Princess Kaliana Benhamed of Ardu Safra and, as such, am expected to marry for the good of my country, my people.'

The room sparked, tension exploding. He looked at her as if seeing her for the first time. Never again would she be Ana to him. She could see it in his eyes, see the shock, the accusation. Her *normal* life was over. Whatever happened next, she could never go back to being a managerial assistant at Charity Resources. She could never have nights out with her friends again, never enjoy the quiet evenings at home with Claire when they'd talked about all sorts of things.

This was the moment her life changed—beyond recognition—for ever. It didn't matter what Rafe's answer was. Her life would change—had already changed.

'You were a virgin that night, no?' he demanded as he moved closer, his dark eyes hard and piercing. *'Dio mio*, Ana, a virgin *and* a princess.'

'Yes, I was,' she snapped indignantly. He

would never understand what was at stake for her right now.

'You never intended to see me again, did you?' There was a hint of feral anger in his voice now. 'Yet here you are. A princess. Offering me, the man who claimed your virginity, a marriage deal.'

The memory of that night became sourer with each word he spoke, each accusing statement. She wanted to turn and leave but her feet wouldn't move, her limbs were frozen. She had to do this, had to finish what she'd started, if she stood any chance of saving the people of Ardu Safra from poverty—saving her father from the shame of financial ruin. If she wanted to avoid a fate worse than death, by marrying Nassif, then she had to make Rafe see this was the best way. For both of them.

'We both need to get married and we know...' She paused as embarrassment rushed over her, obliterating the cool, controlled Princess she was trying to be.

'That we can ignite intense passion between us?' he finished for her, moving closer still, his tall broad shoulders blocking out the light. Her head began to ache. Pressure mounted around her, making her nauseous.

'It's not just that I need to make a marriage for the good of my country. Or even to produce a much-needed heir,' she hastily added, wishing she could step away from him, wishing her body didn't long for his touch, his caress. Wishing she wasn't giving away all that with every breath.

'What else?'

'My family are on the brink of financial ruin. I need a husband. A wealthy man. One who can clear all debts, reinstate stability into our economy.' The truth rushed out and she looked up at him. Waiting.

His eyes scanned her face. Searching for lies. Searching for truth. 'And the Casella fortune that I stand to inherit is your way out?'

She blushed as the shame of it fell over her like the shadow of a storm cloud about to break.

Rafe's eyes darkened, reminding her even more of that night as he moved closer to her.

So close she could almost taste him. 'Give me one good reason why I should marry you.'

'If you don't, I will have to marry a man chosen by my father.' She gulped down the panic just thinking about it induced. 'My wedding is set for October, my twenty-sixth birthday. If I haven't secured a husband by the beginning of September, I must marry Nassif.'

'Nassif?'

'A cruel man, older than me. Widowed.' She looked at Rafe, at the shock on his face. Should she tell him more? 'Uncle of the man I should have married.'

'Why not just say no?'

Her eyes widened in shock. 'I'm a princess. Marriage is my duty.'

'And you think my need to do my family duty will be as strong as your desire to avoid marriage with this Nassif?' The darkness of his eyes had hardened, his expression becoming sterner by the second. His handsome features, which had so captured her imagination that night in London, were hard and angry, showing the true man, she reminded herself, not the man of her wistful dreams.

Panic tore through her. If he didn't want to marry her…? She couldn't bear the thought of having Nassif as her husband. Of sharing with him the kind of intimacies she'd shared with Rafe. She shuddered at the thought.

With a deep breath, she touched the large pearls at her neck, wanting to be free of the clothes she'd chosen for this moment. Wanting to be in London, in her flat, in the life she could no longer have. Her panic increased. If Rafe didn't want to marry her she didn't know what she was going to do.

'And why me?' He moved another step closer, questioning her softly, sending her pulse rate into freefall.

'Because we can offer each other everything needed.' She looked up into his eyes, imploring him to understand. Willing him to accept her deal.

'And our night in London has nothing to do with this?' Suspicion laced through his words like mist in the winter.

'Nothing whatsoever. Although I am certain I'm not the first woman you have taken to your suite within hours of meeting.' The truth of that statement cut like broken glass, shattering the fairy tale of that night for evermore.

Rafe scanned Kaliana's face once more as he tried to push away the image of an older man touching her, when he'd been the first man to show her pleasure. Doubt clouded her eyes, but poise and elegance shone through. He didn't doubt her claim of being a princess. This was a woman in control. She wasn't going to stand by and be dictated to.

He respected that. Still his suspicions persisted. Why him? Why now?

'And if I don't wish to marry you?' Why had he said that when the answer to his dilemma stood deliciously in front of him, offering herself to him, reigniting that flame of desire? That powerful sexual chemistry. How could he be turning down more nights like the one they had shared?

But…marriage?

Her lips parted as his question hit home.

The inviting softness of them reminded him of their lusciousness, of the way they'd tasted of champagne as he'd claimed them in that first demanding kiss at the bar.

'You said you needed to marry.' Her eyes widened, and a smile spread over his lips. She hadn't thought he would refuse. She'd been so sure of herself. A wave of satisfaction at disrupting her plans, her obviously well-prepared speech, surged through him even as he knew he would accept her deal. She was the key to keeping the only thing that mattered to him: Pietra Bianca.

She was the only key.

'Maybe I no longer care what happens to the family name—or the fortune.' He paused as he watched her beautiful face, fighting hard against the urge to reach out and brush his fingers across the softness of her cheeks.

'It would be a marriage we'd both benefit from.'

'I suppose there is the fact that we know we are more than compatible in the bedroom.' He couldn't help taunting her again. Reminding her of what they'd shared.

She flushed, her icy composure knocked once more, the woman he'd met that night shining through like the brightest star.

'That has nothing to do with my proposition.' The star dimmed, sliding behind the clouds of propriety. The aloof Princess who mourned her true love was back in play.

'Are you sure?' He moved forward, reaching out to push back stray strands of hair, wanting to coax out the sex siren.

'Of course it hasn't.' She snapped out the denial, the frosty Princess façade truly on display. 'This is a deal which would benefit us both.'

'That is true.' He paused, his mind lost in another time, another night—another woman. He shut down those thoughts. 'But it will give us the opportunity to explore what still sparks between us.' Again, he taunted her, even knowing what she said made sense. Marriage was the one thing he didn't want. It was also the one thing he would do. For his family. For his mother.

But this woman? She'd already threatened to break through his defences. How was he going to share the intimacies of marriage with her when he already knew he could want her—if he allowed himself to?

'It will be a business deal, Rafe, nothing more.'

No, he couldn't do it. But if he didn't he'd lose the last chance of gaining his father's respect, along with the one thing that held precious memories of his mother. 'And if I don't want such a business deal?'

CHAPTER FOUR

KALIANA PANICKED. SHE hadn't expected the man she'd spent a passionate night with to throw her deal back at her. To virtually be telling her she was mad for even suggesting it. Stupidly, she'd expected him to be grateful to her for offering him a solution to the problem he'd confided to her that night.

She hadn't expected any of this. Hadn't expected the smouldering intensity in his eyes. The heat that just the brush of his fingers on her face could ignite—or the blatant reminder of what they had shared in London that night.

She hadn't thought this through properly. Maybe he'd already found a bride. The thought sent a spike of fear piercing through her. There was so little time left and she'd been so sure he would agree. But it seemed she'd got it all wrong. The thought of marrying Nassif looked like a scary reality.

'I can see I have misjudged things,' she said, stepping away from him as much as the small room would allow. Suddenly she couldn't bear to be close to him. Couldn't bear to be reminded of that night, of how he'd made her feel and think. 'It was wrong of me to assume. I'm sorry I have wasted your time.'

Kaliana turned, reaching out almost blindly to open the door, her heart hammering with hope. Hope that he would tell her to stay. Silence slammed into that futile hope. If he let her go now, she would have to walk away from not only the chance of being free of Nassif, but she would also be walking away from the man who still infused her body with desire. If she had to marry anyone, she would rather it was this man.

The thought of giving herself to any other man was now repulsive to her, but her marriage needed to create children—an heir for Ardu Safra. How could she even contemplate Nassif touching her? How could she endure it, knowing what real passion and desire were?

She closed her eyes against the pain of her situation. The humiliation of what she'd just done. She'd told him something nobody knew, other than Claire. She'd told him who she really was and in doing so had effectively ended the escape of that new life. Her father had made such anonymity possible and if word got out he would revoke that favour. He would insist she return to her life in the country she loved. But it was a country so stuck in the past, in old traditions, she couldn't face living there. Couldn't face being its Princess. She'd always vowed she'd change things, bring everything up to date when she became the Queen, but with Nassif at her side it would be almost impossible.

Time was running out. Fast. She needed a husband.

A wealthy husband.

With a sensation of lead in her stomach she opened the door, the voices of the remaining members of the audience sounding loud and harsh. Rafe wasn't going to stop her. He was going to allow her to walk away. After everything they had shared—or was it because of everything they'd shared?

Kaliana stifled her cry of distress, stepping out of the small office, her head high. The sensation that she was walking into a bleak future was suddenly so real. But she wouldn't look back. Wouldn't give him the satisfaction of seeing her distress, damn him.

'Ana.' He took hold of her hand, bringing her escape to an abrupt halt. Turning, she looked up at him. He was suddenly very close. Too close. Her body responded, the memory of his all too clear in her mind.

'You have made yourself clear. There will be no deal.' She wouldn't let him see her pain, her disappointment. Her panic. 'I hope you find the solution you need.'

His dark eyes held hers, the heaviness in her stomach lightening, becoming a flutter of butterflies. He moved closer still, the intensity in his eyes increasing. He was going to kiss her. She could see it in the darkening of desire in his eyes. She shouldn't let him. Shouldn't want him to.

So why did she? Why did she tilt her chin

up? Why did her breath raggedly slip out and her pulse race? Why did she part her lips so expectantly?

She wanted him to kiss her. Wanted to taste him again—and more. Her body was remembering, the woman she'd been that night resurfacing, even as she tried to keep her cool façade, the demeanour of a princess. It was a futile battle. The Princess she was supposed to be faded fast as that spark, that intense sexual chemistry, swirled round them.

He moved closer still, until they were almost touching and, lowering his head, he brushed his lips over hers. She sighed, pressing herself to him, unwittingly begging for more. Rafe obliged, wrapping her in an embrace so tight her body was fused with his. The slumbering remains of the fire he'd ignited inside her that night in London burst back into life, the flame of desire leaping high, catching her unawares, dragging out the woman he'd awakened.

Kaliana closed her eyes, leaning against him, giving herself up to what she'd been wanting since the moment she'd walked away from him that morning. His touch. His kiss. She slid her hands around his neck, her fingers delving into his hair, passion beginning to consume them. Sweeping them away, making her oblivious to anything around them.

This was what she'd wanted for the last two months. This was what she'd fought so very hard against. This passion. This desire. This man. She kissed him harder as the flames of passion rose up, engulfing her completely. He responded, the intensity of his kiss matching hers.

Rafe moved backwards, still kissing her, his arms wrapped tight around her. She had no option but to move with him back into the room. He kept his arms around her, his body fused to hers, his lips demanding everything from hers. Reaching out, he pushed the door shut. The sudden intimate silence made her gasp against his lips.

They were alone again.

'We haven't finished yet, Ana.' He let go of her, walking away to stand once more in front of the window. Her body felt limp, weakened by his kiss, by being pressed against his body. Weakened by him.

'But I thought…' She struggled to find the words as her heart thumped wildly, the heavy pulse of desire heating her from within.

He turned to face her, anger sparking in his eyes, his jaw tight. 'That you could breeze back into my life, this time as the Princess you really are and not refer to all we shared that night?'

'You need a wife, Rafe.' Kaliana clung to the facts, desperate not to explore the way he made her feel, the excitement of being kissed by him again. Practicalities. That was what she needed to concentrate on. 'And I need a husband.'

'I don't want marriage, Ana, but I *have* to marry, choose a bride. That's why I was drowning my sorrows in whisky that night.' Rafe looked down at her, the war of emotions on his face, in his eyes, all too clear. All too familiar. 'Why should that bride be you, when we know so little of one another?'

'What do you want to know?' She kept her focus even though she couldn't help but smile at him, sensing she'd found a way through his armour. Found a way to make him see this was what they both needed.

'I want to know everything about you, Princess Kaliana, but, more than that, I want to know all about the woman I met in London.'

Rafe saw the smile slip from Kaliana's lips, saw her face pale. The throb of desire from their kiss, a kiss that had been witnessed by many before he'd pushed the door shut, still hummed in his veins. Demanding more. Demanding satisfaction.

'Like what?' The defensive Princess was back in play and he smiled at her prickly demeanour. Now he knew why she'd all but demanded champagne at the bar that night. She was used to the good things in life. Was that why she wanted to make a marriage that would bring wealth to her country? Or was it really her concern for her people? But he had other, far more pressing questions.

'Why did you leave that morning in London? Why did you sneak away before I woke?'

The moment he'd woken to find her gone

had totally knocked him. In the previous hours he'd given so much more of himself to her than he had to any woman. He'd stupidly believed he'd finally met *the woman* but had pushed that aside as his predicament, his duty to his family, had swamped such ideas totally. That and the fact that any woman he'd got close to had slipped out of his life, leaving a void he had never been able to fill.

The coldness of the sheets in the bed had told him she'd long since gone. Had she waited until he'd slept? Waited until the exhaustion of such mind-blowingly hot sex had claimed him?

'Isn't that the protocol for a one-night stand?' Her chin lifted defensively and sparks of irritation verging on anger shone in her eyes, making their dark brown depths a deep gold. She tilted her head coyly to one side, her thick dark hair falling over her shoulder. 'I have never done anything like that before, so if I got it wrong I apologise.'

'*Sì,* sometimes that's the protocol,' he acknowledged, acutely aware that never had a woman slipped from his bed and left him before. He'd always dictated the longevity of an affair, be it hours or weeks. 'But I would like to know—would you have given your virginity to any man that night?'

She blushed and looked down and something crushed him. Hard. Wrapping tight binds around his chest. Standing there in that moment, she looked vulnerable. Alone. Then she looked up, her eyes bright with unshed tears. He became aware of the clock ticking on the wall, marking loudly each passing second as he waited for her answer. He needed to know. Needed to hear that she'd been as drawn to him as he'd been to her. That their night of passion had been fate throwing them together. That it hadn't been contrived. That she had wanted it as much as she'd led him to believe.

'I never set out to spend the night with anyone. A bit of harmless flirting, yes, but not that.' Her whisper was soft. Her face pale. Vulnerability radiated from her so strongly now it was difficult to resist the urge to wrap her up in his life and protect her. 'But something changed...'

Her words trailed off as if she couldn't tell him. Didn't want to admit to anything.

'What changed, Kaliana?' He'd used her full name and it felt good. Right. Slowly he moved closer, unable to help himself. Wanting to be near her, wanting to touch her. Wanting even a hint of evidence that she'd been as consumed by him as he'd been by her.

She shook her head slowly. 'I don't know. It just felt right. Whatever was between us that night, whatever it was that drew us to one another so strongly, was right.'

She blinked hard and he replayed the moments before she'd all but seduced him once more. She'd thought he was a waiter, that he worked in the bar. The truth of that question was as obvious as her innocence had been as he'd claimed it—claimed her. The knowledge satisfied him that her so-called deal was indeed born out of a need to help her country, her people. After all, she could simply refuse to marry this Nassif but, just like him, she couldn't walk away from family duty.

He sighed impatiently, wishing his friend Franco were here right now to help him. To listen to his torrent of questions. But this decision was entirely his to make and he knew Franco would stand by his original advice. A romantic at heart, Franco would be sure to say that if there was an attraction, chemistry, what could go wrong? Was he looking for problems that weren't there? Things he didn't need to worry over? No, he was doing what he usually did when his emotions were threatened. When his defensive barriers were almost breached, as she had subtly begun doing after they'd first made love, asking him for his story, he built them higher. Stronger.

'Is it the Casella fortune or that night which makes me the ideal candidate to be Princess Kaliana's husband?' He couldn't keep the serious tone from his voice, even though he wanted to tease her playfully.

The more he thought about the idea of marriage to her, the more it seemed right. He and Kaliana had shared something amazing that night in London. She'd given him her virginity—a gift he hadn't realised he'd taken until it was too late—so didn't that mean he was the ideal candidate, even without his wealth?

'There is much for us both to gain with this marriage deal.' She moved away from him, calmer now. In control once more. 'In return for your financial support, my family name will, I'm sure, be of use to you in business. Renewable energy is a market ripe for expansion in Ardu Safra and beyond. Our marriage will also be built on the attraction we have for one another. Love isn't required to make it a success.'

'I can't ever promise anything like love,' he said firmly, needing the boundaries around him. Another thought, one more worrying, barged into his mind. 'What if you need more? What if one day you find more with someone else?'

She looked at him firmly. The cool and sophisticated Princess was back in play. The woman he'd met in London had slipped beneath the aloof exterior. 'I have had my chance at love. It hurts to lose it, and I don't need or want that kind of pain in my life. Love is not on the agenda, Rafe. Purely convenience.'

He folded his arms, hating this discussion.

This topic. He'd never discussed such a thing with a woman so openly. 'And what we had that night, the spark of attraction, the sexual chemistry, proves this deal—our marriage—has a chance of working without love?'

'It proves exactly that,' Kaliana said, flushing once more, reminding him of the innocent virgin she'd been as she'd looked at him as he'd claimed her. Made her his.

'And what about children?' He asked the question, hating the answer, hating that his father was pushing him to do just that. He couldn't envisage himself holding a child of his own.

'You have already told me you need a son to continue the Casella name. Don't forget, Rafe, I am a princess. An heir will be expected of our marriage, but...' her voice trailed off and mischief sparkled in her eyes '...if you object to that, I understand.'

Object? To another night like that night in London? Was she serious? 'I have no objection,' he said far more calmly than he felt. He certainly didn't object to more hot sex with Kaliana, but he did object to the idea of fa-

thering a child. Fear of being as cold and un-
loving as his father had cemented that idea
in his mind long ago and now duty to his father, his family, meant he had to find a way
to get past that.

'Then you accept my deal?'

He didn't know what to say, didn't know
how to answer. All he knew was that if he allowed her to walk away again he'd regret it.
Whatever it was between them wasn't over
yet. Wasn't finished. And if it meant entering
into a marriage deal, one that would enable
him to keep Pietra Bianca safe and maybe
even please his father, be the better son, then
he would do it.

After all, marriages could be broken. Ended.

'Very well. I accept your deal.'

The relief on her face made him smile. She
was as desperate to make this marriage as he
was. But he wasn't done yet. She'd made her
terms very clear, but he had some of his own
to bring to the table.

'I do, however, have terms of my own.' Rafe's
words left Kaliana speechless for a few sec-

onds, tension filling her. He couldn't do this to her. Couldn't make demands now. Not after kissing her like that. Making such a scene as he'd all but dragged her back into the room, passion gripping them both. She blushed at the thought of how it must have looked. Like lovers who needed to get a room. Like they must have looked at the bar in London. She blushed at the memory.

Finally, she found her voice, but it was more of a stutter as uncertainty gripped her. 'What conditions?'

'I am a Sicilian. And we are a proud lot.' Humour weaved into his voice, lifting the tension. He looked so handsome, so irresistible. His dark eyes sparkled, his lips curving into that sexy smile.

She almost laughed as the mood lightened, becoming more like the time they'd spent together in London. 'I had worked that much out.'

His eyes fixed to hers, questioning if she was making fun of him. Seriousness took over once again, making Kaliana feel dizzy from the seesawing emotions. 'And I will not have anyone think I am marrying as part of a deal.'

'Is that why you just kissed me? In front of those people out there?' The questions rushed from her before she could stop them. 'To make it look like we are lovers?'

'No, Kaliana.' He smiled, that sinfully sexy smile he'd used in the bar of the hotel in London making her heart flutter as the zap of attraction rushed over her once more. What would it be like if he'd kissed her because he wanted to? She held her breath as he moved a little closer, his expression dark and serious. 'I kissed you because I wanted to.'

Kaliana's tummy flipped over. He had wanted to kiss her. Just as she had wanted him to. And she'd kissed him back with as much fervour as he'd kissed her. 'What are your conditions?'

'I do need to marry, yes, that is very true. I can also relieve the financial pressures your country faces. But I will not have it said we married out of necessity. I don't want anyone to know this is a deal brokered between us.

After our little floor show just now, I'm sure the tongues are already wagging.'

'That's what I'm afraid of.' If word got out just who she was, any chance of living quietly until her wedding day would be over. She'd be forced to take on the role of a princess, might even be forced to return to Ardu Safra, where she would have guards assigned and be unable to be herself. To be free. She didn't want her children growing up locked away from reality as she had been.

'It's exactly what we need.' Rafe's words brought her hurtling back to the reality of this moment. The reality of brokering a marriage deal with Raffaele Casella.

'Why, Rafe? Why do we need that?'

'If we are to marry, I want everyone to think it is because we want to do so. I want people to believe it's real. Believe we are in love. A whirlwind romance, no?' Kaliana's heart pounded as he said those last words. Love was what she still secretly desired but she was scared in case it couldn't happen twice in a lifetime. Mentally she shook herself. Whatever this was between her and Rafe, it was more like lust.

'Why would you want to do that?' Nerves made her voice quiver.

'I have spent all my adult life avoiding the state of matrimony. I told myself I never wanted to succumb to the dangerous emotion of love. My family and friends know this, so we need to convince them otherwise.'

'And you are a man who doesn't want to let love into his life?' They were more suited than he knew, but the look on his face told her she'd spoken the truth. For whatever reason, Rafe refused to let love into his heart or his life.

'How well you already know me. But what about you? Do you seek love in your life?' He walked away from her, back towards the window, giving her much-needed breathing space. At least she could think more clearly now without her heart pounding so loudly.

'No.' The word snapped from her. Was she trying to convince herself? Or Rafe? She was already dangerously drawn to him. Already he was making her forget Alif. Forget all they'd had. But what would happen if he crept into her heart? If she began to feel something for him? She pushed the questions aside. 'I have known love once and that is enough. I don't seek it any more.'

'*Bene.* Then I suggest we go out there and show everyone how we feel about each other.'

'How we feel?' The mischief in his eyes did terrible things to her. Made clear and concise thought impossible.

'That we are mad for one another.' He smiled at her and her stomach flipped over, tingles of pleasure rushing through her.

CHAPTER FIVE

LATER THAT EVENING, Rafe had stood at her side as she'd called her father, his official request for her hand in marriage met with unexpected enthusiasm.

'Kaliana and I are both duty-bound to make a marriage that will benefit our families and I would like to ask you for your daughter's hand in marriage.' Rafe's strong and determined voice had filled her with confidence. Everything was going to be all right.

'It's not the woman,' her father had said, the ruler he'd become booming loudly down the phone. 'You also marry the kingdom. Are you man enough for that?'

'I most certainly am.' Rafe's confident reply had made her smile and now, over a week later, as they sat having lunch outside a small restaurant, she couldn't help but smile at the memory of it.

His brows flicked upwards as he saw her smiling. 'You have a beautiful smile.'

'I was thinking about the way you all but told Father we were getting married.' She hid her confused embarrassment at the compliment. 'I just hope your father is as pleased when I meet him this afternoon.'

'He will be.' Rafe glanced at the other couples having lunch, all of them more interested in them than their food. 'It seems our news has travelled fast.'

'Sadly, yes. My cover has been blown and now I have to be Princess Kaliana.' She sighed. 'Which means I have to give up the life I'd made in London.'

'It had to happen. Whoever you married, that life could never be part of it. Even I know that.' Rafe genuinely sounded remorseful and she smiled as he settled the bill. 'Before we see my father, I'd like to take you somewhere quiet. Somewhere that will give us time and space to get to know one another a little better.'

Kaliana looked across at him. Time to be alone with Rafe was what she'd hoped for all week. What she'd yearned for like a lovestruck teenager. 'I'd like that.'

When they returned to his car, a soft laugh escaped her, one born of nerves. 'It's not easy getting to know the man I'm going to marry when we are always acting the romantic couple just because we are being watched. I'd like to get to know you better. The real you.'

He looked at her, seriousness filling his eyes, his dark, demanding gaze holding hers. The ever-present tension ramped up around them, the interior of his sleek car becoming far too confining.

'You want to get to know me?' Surprise filled his voice and a delicious sense of anticipation slipped over her. It didn't last long. 'Do you not know all you need to know?'

Kaliana swallowed back her surprise. He was reminding her that this was just a deal. This wasn't real. And whatever foolish sentiments were in her mind she'd do well to keep them to herself because she was in danger of reading too much into every smile, every caress, every kiss.

'Of course.' She kept her voice light, her

smile disguising her shock. Her disappointment. She focused her attention in front of her, willing him to start driving. To stop looking at her. She needed to get her wayward thoughts in order, back into the mindset that this was just a deal and could never be anything else.

Each date they'd been on last week had proved to her she'd done the right thing. That together they made a good team. That they could both fulfil the requirements of their families with their marriage. And maybe she could have part of her secret wish and at least they could be happy together. Something she couldn't envisage happening with Nassif.

Not once had she and Rafe talked intimately. Not once had they shared who they really were. Kaliana knew she was guilty of hiding behind barriers and defensive walls. So, was it the same for Rafe? Was he using their role play of romance and his family duty as a barrier?

'Then I know the perfect place,' he said, turning his attention to manoeuvring the car into the traffic.

Within seconds they were in the flow of traffic, heading out of Palermo. She glanced across at him; his eyes were rigidly fixed on the road ahead. As if he didn't dare look at her. As if he could sense her gradually changing feelings towards him.

'Somewhere peaceful we can talk sounds perfect.' She couldn't help the small sigh of satisfaction at the thought. 'Just talk and get to know one another.'

'Better than we got to know one another in London?' This time he did glance across at her and that teasing sparkle filled his eyes. She never knew where she stood with him. Was that his way of keeping this arrangement purely that? His way of preventing it from ever coming anywhere near something more meaningful?

Kaliana's breath shuddered from her. She wanted to look away, wanted to hide herself from him, but she couldn't.

Instead she laughed. 'Raffaele Casella, you are incorrigible.' Then she turned to look out of the window, hiding the flush spreading over her cheeks. What was the matter with her?

She watched the view of the sparkling sea as they drove along the coast road. Anything other than look at him and give into the fizz of attraction which hummed through her. It sizzled in the air around them. Waiting to explode.

Rafe's silence continued as they turned off the coast road and began driving along narrow twisting lanes. It all looked so beautiful, but Kaliana couldn't speak. Her throat was dry, her nerves on edge. Was this what being alone with him would be like?

'Am I really incorrigible?' he asked, teasing her from her silence as he pulled the car off the road.

She turned to look at him, trying to beat down the intensity of her feelings. Sensations she couldn't put a name to. 'Yes, you are.' She smiled, unable to help herself be anything but charmed by him. By his sexy smile. She arched a brow upwards, feeling as flirtatious as she had that night in the bar.

He looked at her, the silence heavy, and she

lowered her gaze, then looked up from beneath her lashes. 'I like that about you.'

Her gaze locked with his, her heart thudding wildly in her chest. So much so that when he glanced lower she was sure he must be able to see her pulse thumping at the base of her throat. 'Why are we here, Rafe?' she asked, needing to change the subject.

She had to get out of the confines of the car. Away from the scent of the man she'd given herself to with complete abandon, believing it would be her only chance at finding such pleasure.

Now she was about to marry him.

Except this version of Rafe wasn't the man she'd met that night. That man was as much of an enigma as she had been. They'd lost themselves with such abandon that night, and she certainly hadn't expected to see him again. Much less be preparing to marry him.

'We are here to learn more about each other,' he said, his voice husky as he looked into her eyes, making her pulse thump ever harder. 'This is what you want, is it not, *cara mia*?'

* * *

'Here?' Kaliana teased him with a smile and Rafe gritted his teeth against the hot spark of lust hurtling straight to his groin. How could this woman make him feel like this? How could his desire for her still be so strong? Unquenched?

Because you still want her. The voice of reason slammed into him. *You couldn't get enough of her that night, weren't ready to end the encounter, but she walked out on you.*

He smiled, trying to lighten the mood. Trying to push away those damning thoughts. He had to get out of the car. Had to get away from her before he did something stupid like kiss her. Again. There was no way he was going to allow her to know she had any kind of power over him. At least not sexual power.

'This is Pietra Bianca. It was my mother's land,' he said, turning the engine off, the silence suddenly heavy around them.

'I can tell it's very special to you.' Kaliana looked across at him, unnerving him with her ability to see what he didn't want her to see.

'It's a place full of memories. Happy memories of a childhood with Enzo.' She was doing it again. Slipping under that defensive barrier he'd built around himself. Dragging him out. Exposing his innermost emotions.

'Are you sure you want to be here today?' she questioned slowly. Tentatively.

'*Sì.*' He grappled with English briefly as the urge to reach across the car and stroke his fingers down her cheek almost took over. Instead he opened the door, the August heat rushing into the air-conditioned interior. A heat that nowhere near matched the hot desire as he'd answered the primal call Kaliana's body had made to his in the hotel bar that night. Heat and desire that was still very much alive. That kiss at the charity event had proved that. A week of very public dates hadn't lessened it. The inability to touch her, hold her, kiss her, as he had done that first night, only intensifying his need. His desire.

All week he'd played the role he'd dictated. Courted the press. Showed off their romance. And it had worked. His father and even Enzo were on board with his choice of wife and mother of the heir they all needed.

He and Kaliana had crossed the first hurdle—gained family acceptance on both sides and created a buzz about their relationship. The next step was to get to know one another better. Which was why he'd brought her here. To the peace and quiet of the place that meant the most to him.

It was the one piece of land belonging to the Casella family which he needed to keep. The reason he'd bowed to pressure from his father and agreed to marry. Pietra Bianca had to remain in Casella hands.

'It's a pretty place,' she said, opening her door, stepping out, giving him a view of her long, lean denim-clad legs, which had wrapped around him so perfectly. Rafe refused to remember. Refused to be drawn by the desire she obviously could still evoke.

He hadn't been able to keep his eyes off Kaliana when she'd stepped out of her house that morning in jeans which hugged her hips to perfection and a navy loose-fitting blouse which she wore deliciously low, reminding him, if he'd needed it, just how perfect her breasts were. *Dio mio*, she still looked as sexy as hell. Still as hard to resist.

'There is a special place I would like you to see, and I thought a picnic in the olive groves would be the perfect spot to talk.' He paused and looked at the woman who was to be his bride. 'In private, before we make our romance, our engagement, official.'

He'd had the idea of bringing Kaliana out here when he'd decided to visit the olive and lemon groves his mother had loved so much. He wasn't sure why, but for some reason he needed Kaliana to see the place that was so special to him.

'Are you trying to be romantic with me, Rafe Casella?' Again that flirtatious and teasing voice lured him back towards desire, away from the pain of the past, away from the agony of losing his mother.

'Romance is not something I usually indulge in,' he said sternly, trying to control the rush of desire just being with her evoked. Too sternly if the look of shock on Kaliana's pretty face was anything to go by. 'I simply thought we could get to know one another better. It will make our *love affair* more convincing.'

'What do you want to know?' Caution sounded in her voice and he sensed her reservations.

'Things that will convince anyone we are in love,' he said, moving towards her, her eyes full of the same swirling desire he'd seen in the bar as she'd seduced him. Whatever it was between them, it was still vibrantly alive.

'I need to know more than where you like to be kissed, Kaliana.'

He couldn't help adding that taunt, his voice rising on the last few words, making it obvious he was teasing her again. He watched her eyes darkening, reminding him of when she'd looked at him in the bar just moments before she'd kissed him that first time.

That kick of lust threatened to unleash itself again and he stepped back, his feet crunching the gravel as he did so. Hell, if he didn't control himself he'd want to make her his again. Right here and now.

'Maybe I don't like to be kissed,' she said in a brisk but husky voice as she put much-

needed distance between them by walking towards the olive trees. Towards the place that
was so special to him—a place he'd never
told any woman about, let alone shown, but
Kaliana deserved to see it. After all, their
marriage would keep it in the Casella family. Keep it for his children.

Rafe took the basket his housekeeper had
prepared from the car and, with a carefree
smile which didn't match the way he felt,
looked at Kaliana. 'This way.'

At first she seemed uncertain, then she followed him, her flat shoes at least suitable for
the gravel path which led towards the place
he'd enjoyed so much before his world had
been turned upside down by his mother's
death.

Slowly they walked down through the
gnarled old olive trees; as a young boy he'd
found interesting things buried in the dusty
earth beneath them. As a man, in a desperate
attempt to keep the land from being developed by his father, he had set about making
such finds known. For now, Pietra Bianca
was safe—but only if he married Kaliana.

Only then could he keep the memories of his mother alive.

'I'm surprised this hasn't been developed into one of those luxury complexes the Casellas are so famous for,' Kaliana said, looking about her as she walked at his side. She'd obviously done further research on him and his family since the charity event.

'My business interests do not include developing places like this. I am not of the same mind as my father or, indeed, my brother.' Rafe's tone was clipped and short as he recalled his father's fury when he'd refused to agree to be part of the impressive Casella business after university. Instead he'd told his father he wanted to forge his own way, create his own empire. Something his mother had backed him on, but sadly she hadn't lived to see it being fulfilled.

'Renewable energy, isn't it?' Kaliana asked as they reached a small stone house. He stopped, looking at her. She smiled, her eyes alive with triumph. 'You didn't think I'd marry you without learning something more about you, did you?'

'I assume that was to ensure I was wealthy enough in my own right to enable you to solve your country's financial problems.' The truth and reality of why he was even standing here with her now hit home. It was all about money for her and, for him, possessions.

'If you are so annoyed with that, why did you agree to marry me?' Annoyance sparked in each word, like flint on a stone.

'I have no other option. Like you, I am bound by family tradition. Honour.' He couldn't keep the bitterness from his voice. Enzo's misfortune had become his too. 'Your deal was the solution to my problem. As you so rightly said, we both stand to gain from the arrangement.'

'Duty is what drives us both, Rafe. Duty and honour.' Anger simmered in her sharp retort, stoking his own annoyance at the situation.

'More so in your case. Your country is at stake.' His words rushed out before he could filter them, strip them of the raw emotion just talking about this evoked. 'You are a princess. I'm an ordinary man.'

She turned to look at him as he stated the obvious, her hair swinging as she did so, brushing her shoulders. Even now, in the depths of the real reason they were marrying, she tempted him.

'I still feel there is another motive,' she said carefully, watching him suspiciously as they stood in the shade of the stone house. 'Another reason for agreeing to my deal.'

He drove his fingers into his hair, dragging his hand back over his scalp. She was right, and if he wanted to learn more about her, then didn't he need to give away details of his personal history?

'In my grandfather's time the Casella name nearly ended.' How could he explain all the complications of his family? 'My father is terminally ill and will not rest until he knows I am married and a father—to a son. He even insisted I undertook fertility tests to ensure Enzo's fate wasn't also mine. Not for me, but for the Casella name.'

'He made you do that?' The angry tension slipped back a notch, leaving him more relaxed. More open to such a discussion. To sharing secrets.

'Yes.' Just thinking how much his life had altered in the last few months brought anger rushing back to the surface.

Rafe could still feel the shock as his father had told him of Enzo's predicament— a problem that radiated far further than just Enzo and Emma's marriage. Rafe had been too blinded by the pain he knew Emma would be feeling to even worry what sort of implications the revelation had on him. On his life. His future.

A future which he should have shared with Emma. He would have, if Enzo hadn't competed for her so determinedly, taking away the only woman Rafe had loved. He'd stood back as they had married. Allowed his love for her to wilt and die and now, as their marriage threatened to fall apart, all he could feel was sympathy for Emma, who'd wanted children so much. After all, when they had been together, even for that short time, she'd made it clear that being a mother was something she really wanted.

It wasn't until their father had all but demanded Rafe have a fertility test to ensure that at least one of the twins would be able to father the next Casella generation that Rafe realised the implications for him.

'That's terrible.' Kaliana finally found a voice, pressing her fingertips to her lips and right there, at that moment, he wished he was kissing her, tasting her lips, instead of having this conversation. It was safer.

'Naturally, my father was more concerned about the continuation of the Casella name than Enzo's floundering marriage, or even the fact that Enzo had married the woman I once loved. So you can rest assured that our marriage will produce the children that both our families expect of us.'

Kaliana's eyes had widened, filling with disbelief at Rafe's confession of his father's actions. Not that it mattered now. His father was mercenary, and love meant nothing to him. Why else would he have made his own wife's life so unhappy? Even as she'd been seriously ill, Rafe's mother had tried to defend the man she loved. Tried to convince

Rafe it was just his father's way. That, deep down, he loved her and his twins. Both of them—equally.

No, Rafe would never believe that.

'You don't want children, do you? Given the choice, that is.' The words were a whisper. A shocked whisper.

He couldn't lie to her. But he couldn't tell her how he feared being the same as his father had been to him. Cold and indifferent. 'No, given the choice, I don't. I don't want to be married either but, like you, having lost someone I loved, I'm doing so.'

'At least I know where I stand.' Kaliana's voice struggled beneath the heaviness of his honesty. Had he done the right thing being so brutal? So honest? Yes. He couldn't allow her to form any attachment to him. Not when he was so unworthy of love. When every person he'd ever loved had rejected him—or worse.

'This marriage, our marriage, is one we are making because of duty to our families. Not a marriage made with the promise of love and happy ever after. It is a marriage for financial gain—for both of us.' He forced home his point, reminding her of the real reason they were doing this. Reminding himself.

If he pushed her too hard, might she walk away? Might she free him of this deal, his duty? Was that why he was being so mercenary? So like his damn father? Because, deep down, he wanted to be free?

'You sound very bitter about love, Rafe, and happy-ever-afters. What happened?' Kaliana walked slowly towards him, her hands clasping her arms, hugging herself, as if she too felt the change in the atmosphere around them.

'I'm just being practical. And honest.' Rafe needed to redirect the conversation. In such a short time she had dug deep into his soul, opening old wounds, the kind of wounds he'd refused to deal with any more.

She shook her head in silent agreement, one hand rubbing the top of her arm in a gesture of comfort he so wished he could give her. But right now the past had been painfully exhumed and spread out before him and all he wanted to do was run from it.

'As practical as your father was when he

insisted you have that test?' In one sharp sentence she'd ploughed deep into his insecurities. Passing that test had been the one thing he'd done right as far as his father was concerned.

'*Sì,*' he said, distracted by memories. 'And what of your father? Is he happy with the marriage deal you have brokered? Will he be happy when he meets me?' He took it back to basics. Away from anything resembling emotion, even though he knew from his own father that Kaliana's was more than happy.

'Very much so.' She lifted her chin a little, the sunlight dancing in her hair. 'Wedding preparations are already underway.' She narrowed her eyes. 'Your father is not opposed to our marriage, I take it? Even though I am not Sicilian?'

'He too is happy,' Rafe said, recalling the conversation he'd had with his father about the marriage deal. His reaction to his son marrying a princess had been nothing short of overjoyed. Not only would the Casella name continue, but it would do so with royal blood in its veins. Rafe had excelled himself.

Earnt his respect. 'You will see that for yourself very soon. All we need to do is continue with the pretence of a whirlwind romance.'

She nodded, walking slowly away from him, pretending to look around her, pretending none of this bothered her. 'I guess it is.' She turned, smiling. 'Did you say something about a picnic earlier?' Her voice was so light and carefree it was hard to believe they'd just been discussing something so difficult for both of them.

He smiled, enjoying her sensitivity. Marriage to Kaliana wasn't going to be a hardship, but then it wasn't the marriage he'd once envisaged as a young man. When he'd fallen in love for the first time.

'I did and I know just the spot.' He took her hand, forcing his smile to brighten. 'This way.'

Kaliana's mind filled with worry and she struggled to disguise it. The fact that Rafe needed her as his wife should have made her feel less anxious, less worried he might back out. But she could sense his hesitation, his reluctance. This was a man who went out of his way to avoid emotional commitment His admission of losing the woman he'd loved to his brother had proved that.

Maybe that was the best way. She'd had her chance at real romance, real love and happy ever after. A marriage based on sexual chemistry, one which solved the issues her country faced, was safer emotionally.

'This is where I used to picnic with my mother,' Rafe said as they reached a gentle downward slope dotted with ancient gnarled olive trees. A low stone wall, old and crumbling, stood in the middle of the small clearing, the afternoon sun streaming between the leaves creating a totally magical scene.

The beauty of the spot was overshadowed by his words. This was the first time Rafe had mentioned his mother and she wasn't going to allow the chance to pass, knowing from her recent research on him that he'd lost his mother when he was in his late teens. 'Do you miss her?'

'I was seventeen when she died. Almost a man, but still too young to lose a mother. I hope my child never has to experience such pain, such loss.' It was as if he'd forgotten himself. As if she wasn't there. Or at least not Kaliana, his bride-to-be.

'It must have been awful,' she said, instinctively reaching out to touch his arm.

Rafe looked at her, but she knew he was lost in the heartache of all he'd endured. 'Nothing was as bad as losing my mother, not even being the second-best son in my father's eyes.'

He paused, caught between the past and the present. He slipped backwards. 'My mother suddenly became very ill and when she died I lost my ally in life.' From the look on his face, she guessed this wasn't something he talked much about, was something he guarded well.

'Your father must have been beside himself.'

'My father never showed emotion. I don't know what he felt, but after my mother's death he became even harder to please.' His eyes became dark and thunderous. 'The only thing I ever did right since that day was pass that damned fertility test.'

Kaliana didn't know what to say, instinctively reaching out to touch his arm. He looked down at her hand on his shirt sleeve then up to her face. 'Oh, Rafe.' Her heart ached for the teenager who'd lost his mother so tragically. 'You did your best.'

'But it wasn't enough.' He shook his head, pressing his lips together as he reined in the anger sparking in his eyes. 'That's when I knew I didn't want to be a father.'

'But now? You need a child, an heir. We both do.' The words slipped from her lips so fast she couldn't check them, couldn't keep the thought to herself.

Rafe looked at her and for a moment, in the dappled light of the olive groves, he looked like the man she'd met in London. But then the sun slipped behind a cloud and the moment was gone. Now he was Raffaele Casella. The man who'd calmly agreed to her deal for a marriage of convenience.

'I know my duty, Kaliana. I can assure you our child will want for nothing.'

'What about love?' She could manage without love in her life, but she wanted her child to be loved—by both parents. If he couldn't do that, it was almost a deal-breaker. Almost because she had little choice now. The wheels of their deal had been put in motion. Time was running out. 'Can you love your children?'

Rafe's eyes narrowed in that way he did when he didn't believe her, didn't trust her. 'Love is the one thing I can no longer give. Not to anyone.'

The starkness of that statement, the total indifference in it, set off alarms in her mind, made questions race.

'Children?' Rafe spoke again before she could form her response to his declaration. 'You want more than one?'

Kaliana looked at Rafe, insecurities from her own childhood surfacing. She should have been a son, the one thing her mother had never truly got over. Her father's adoration for her hadn't been enough to ease her mother's worry that no further babies blessed their marriage. 'Yes, Rafe, children. I am a princess. An only child. I need to have children. My country needs heirs.'

'Hell, Kaliana, if that doesn't make us sound like pawns in their games, I don't know what does.' His angry outburst shocked her. Shocked him too. He looked at her as he sat on the picnic blanket, the innocence of the setting making the context of their conversation even more powerful. Even more scary.

'Our first child may be a boy,' she said flatly, trying to remember this was a deal. Not a real marriage. They were not like a normal couple talking through how many children they wanted. They would never be a normal couple. 'An heir to continue the Casella name and an heir for Ardu Safra.'

He moved closer. Very close. The mood of the moment had changed as quickly as the desert wind. 'I'm looking forward to creating that baby.' His voice was soft, every syllable caressing her. Stoking the desire she'd been suppressing since that kiss at the charity event.

Birds chattered in the trees around them, cicadas chirped and Kaliana's mind whirled, her body shimmering with heat which had nothing to do with the hot sunshine. Rafe reached out to touch her face and Kaliana held her breath as he gently brushed her windswept hair from her face. 'Making that obligatory heir will not be a hardship, no?'

'Don't,' she whispered, wanting to get away, wanting to move back from his touch. 'Everything is so complicated.'

'*Dio mio*, complicated isn't the right description. But this can save us.' He caressed her cheek with the backs of his fingers. 'This passion, this desire, can distract us.'

'Can it?'

'It's still there, Kaliana, that connection. That chemistry. You can feel it too, can't you?' His voice was husky, the caress of his thumb against her cheek hard to ignore. So hard to resist. But she had to; she couldn't allow herself to dream. To hope.

'It's just lust,' she said quickly, horrified at how husky her voice had become.

'You want me, no?' How could she admit that when it would give him all the power?

'No.' The indignant word shot from her lips.

'If I kiss you now, your heart rate won't speed up? Your breath won't catch in your throat? And your eyes won't darken until they look like the midnight sky? Just as they did when you kissed me in London.'

'Stop it.'

He laughed. 'I don't think you really want me to, do you, Kaliana?'

She lifted her chin defiantly. 'Then kiss me so I can prove you wrong.'

His lips lifted into a slow sexy smile, his pupils enlarging, darkening his eyes as his fingers brushed back and forth on her cheek. Just as he'd claimed, her pulse raced. Her breath caught audibly in her throat and she was sure her eyes were giving away everything.

'Very well, *cara*, I will kiss you.'

She smelt the delicious citrus tang of his aftershave as he brushed his lips over hers, forcing her eyes closed as the onslaught of desire stampeded over her. She dragged in a long ragged breath, waiting for his arms to hold her, waiting to feel his body against hers. She wanted all that and more.

He drew back. 'I think that proves my point.'

She blinked rapidly in shock, unable to stand the smug satisfaction on his face. Anger raged through her, mixing with the heady pulse of desire that light touch of his lips had ignited once more. 'That proves nothing.'

'It proves you want me. It proves what we had in London is still very much alive.'

'But that's not what our deal, our marriage, is about.'

'We can make it about whatever we like.' The suggestion in those dark and sexy eyes was all too clear.

Kaliana wanted to believe him. Wanted more nights like that night which seemed so long ago now. Like a dream which had dimmed over time. The weight of the afternoon's discussion lifted as he smiled at her, taking her right back to that moment in the bar in London. The moment she'd known he would be the man she'd give herself to.

'How can I say no?'

'You can't,' he said, gently bringing her against him.

She lifted herself onto her tiptoes, brushing her lips over his, the fight she'd been trying to keep alive in her body slipping away as the need to kiss him took over. 'I don't want to either.'

Rafe squeezed Kaliana's hand as they entered Villa Casella later that afternoon. The potent kiss they'd shared had broken the tension between them, but he still sensed her apprehension at meeting his father. 'It will be fine.'

She looked up at him and he could almost forget this was an arrangement. For that moment it was as if something real drew and held them together. Something more than just convenience. More than sexual chemistry.

'Okay,' she said, pressing her lips together. 'Let's do this.'

The sensation of reality evaporated.

'Father, this is Kaliana,' Rafe said as his father met them on the terrace.

'*Sì*, the Princess. *Benvenuto*.' He embraced Kaliana warmly and Rafe saw the relief on her face. It really mattered that he accepted her. His father let Kaliana go and looked at him. 'You will, of course, have the engagement party here. I cannot yet travel.'

'It will be here,' Kaliana said without even glancing at him for approval. 'Especially as the wedding will have to be in Ardu Safra.'

'And what of your preparations for the big day?' he asked and Rafe watched, bemused, as his father took an interest. Had he finally done something that pleased his father? Earnt his respect?

'It's going well, thank you,' Kaliana said with a smile.

'And Franco?' His father turned his attention to Rafe. 'Is he to be your best man?'

'He is,' Rafe said and looked at Kaliana. 'In fact, we will be flying to Rome for a few days to meet him and his wife, Francesca.'

'We are?' Kaliana asked, looking up at him with astonishment.

'Franco is looking forward to meeting you, as is his wife.' Rafe had little choice. After all the support Franco had given since he'd first met Kaliana, getting his bride and friend together was something he needed to do.

'Then I guess we are,' Kaliana said, laughing conspiratorially with his father, and Rafe found himself looking forward to a few days—and nights—in Kaliana's company.

CHAPTER SIX

THEIR ARRIVAL IN Rome had created a fresh
flurry of interest from the world's press but
Rafe's luxury apartment gave him and Kaliana the peace they sought. Rafe had watched
as Kaliana marvelled at the ornate painted
ceilings and the vastness of the three-storey
apartment.

'This place is amazing.' Kaliana turned,
smiling at him, looking more relaxed than
he'd ever seen her.

'It is pretty special,' Rafe said, amused at
her pleasure at the classical Italian architec-
ture. 'And perfect to enjoy some peace. An
escape from all those curious eyes.'

Kaliana frowned, a serious expression slipping over her face. 'Where will we live once
we are married?'

Rafe had barely given a thought to the logistics of their marriage. He'd been so focused on achieving all he and the Casella family needed from their union that their future as a married couple hadn't demanded any of his attention.

'I am often in London on business. I see no reason why we cannot spend some time there. We are making a marriage that is more convenient to our families than us.'

Kaliana flinched at his words. Had he been too honest? Too brutal?

'Would that really work?' she asked firmly, then smiled as if trying to return to the teasing lightness of moments ago. 'Between each of our commitments in our homelands, it will be difficult for us to be together much.'

Had she read his mind? Or was that what she wanted?

'Something else we will have to work out. But first we need to continue the show of our whirlwind romance and to do that you need an engagement ring before we meet Franco and Francesca this evening.' Rafe spoke his thoughts aloud as he watched the woman who would soon be his wife walk across their suite to look out over Rome.

Her shoulder-length hair bobbing jauntily reminded him of the time it had fallen in a curtain around her face as he'd made her his that first night. A night he hoped would be repeated. He'd never experienced such a strong attraction to a woman. Not even Emma had fired such an intense desire through his veins. At least that part of his deal with Kaliana was right.

Kaliana turned from surveying the view of the city. She didn't speak, but the arch of her brow left him in no doubt she was still annoyed at him for insisting they put on such an act as part of their deal. Her silence had hummed with annoyance as he'd watched her, her sexy figure highlighted in the late-summer sunshine lighting the room.

That annoyance was still palpable as she looked at him, that haughty air he couldn't help but find sexy radiating from her. 'A ring that is also part of the act?' Her quick reply fired back at him.

He walked towards her, determined to thaw

her increasingly icy mood. 'A ring that will seal our deal, *mia cara.*'

She lifted her chin, looking up at him, challenge clearly in her eyes.

'And there I was thinking we were in Rome for a romantic week together. That you wanted to rekindle the passion between us.' Her flippant reply, laced with seductive teasing, made it almost impossible to suppress his laughter. He couldn't yet understand why just being with Kaliana, even when she challenged him, made him want to laugh.

She made him feel carefree in a way he hadn't felt since he'd lost Emma to his brother. Just as she had that first night, Kaliana made him believe he could have more. That he was worthy of love. That if he could let go of the past, she was the one who would unlock his heart. He could almost believe something meaningful could grow between them—if only he opened himself to the possibility.

But could he trust that instinct, that elusive sensation, when he'd got it so wrong once before?

Whatever it was, Kaliana was the perfect

antidote to Enzo's betrayal and the situation he now faced. The standby heir forced to perform like a stud horse. Forced to step up to his duty.

'Those were the terms of our arrangement, Kaliana. It is what we agreed.' Mentioning the word arrangement pushed those far-fetched ideas from his mind. Romance was the last thing he needed. And love was the one thing he didn't want. Such emotions destroyed you. Left you vulnerable to pain. Disappointment.

At least he and Kaliana were on the same page. She wasn't harbouring notions of love and those non-existent happy-ever-afters. He could still recall her now, full of confidence, as she'd claimed she'd had her chance at love. That she didn't want to find it again.

'Naturally I wish to show off my fiancée. I want the world to see the beautiful woman I am to marry.'

'Then we had better get the biggest ring possible,' she taunted him, that wicked glint of mischief in her eyes sending fire hurtling through him. 'Make sure it's flashy and bold enough to leave no one in doubt.'

'If that's what you want, then so be it.' He entered into her game, the memory of the outcome of that seductive game she'd first played with him so fresh it was as if it had just happened. As if time had been turned back.

Rafe laughed. 'I can see our marriage will be entertaining at the very least.'

He kept that thought with him as he sat in one of Rome's most exclusive jewellers, an array of glittering rings before them. The staff were falling over themselves to get what Kaliana wanted and she was certainly doing as she'd threatened, demandingly ensuring she got the biggest and flashiest ring.

His mind raced back to the night she'd arrived in the bar, demanding champagne. How could he have been so stupid not to have realised she was a woman of such high calibre? Such breeding. A woman who demanded her exacting standards to be met. Did the version of Kaliana he'd walked among the olive groves with last weekend really exist? The woman whose lips he'd brushed with his.

Tasting passion and desire as well as her fight to conceal it.

This sexy, spirited vision of confidence was the real Kaliana. Not at all the kind of woman he'd envisioned would one day become his wife once he'd accepted marriage was something he couldn't avoid. He'd always thought that woman would be soft, gentle and kind. Like his mother. A woman who would be able to heal his wounds and show him how to love. Give him the confidence to set his heart free from its prison.

Was that Kaliana? Sometimes. But right now she was exactly what he needed if he was to keep Pietra Bianca and prevent his cousin and her greedy husband from taking the Casella fortune and adding it permanently to the Romano name. No matter what else happened, he wanted that.

'What about this one?' Kaliana held her hand out, showcasing a small subtle ring on her long slender finger.

'An excellent choice,' the assistant said. 'The vintage raspberry tourmaline and diamond is quite stunning and so delicate.'

'It's not what I expected you to select.' Her earlier threat of buying the biggest ring possible rang in his ears. She'd been toying with him. Like a cat who had just brought in a mouse.

She smiled at him, softness lighting her eyes like the first rays of sun at dawn. 'This one would be my choice.'

'I thought you wanted a statement ring.' Rafe watched her with mock suspicion.

She laughed. 'That's not me, Rafe.' She looked down at the ring on her finger. 'But this is.'

'Then that is the one.' Her smile, her genuine pleasure at the dainty ring dragged him back to the place where he could almost wish it was real. Wish they were getting engaged for love.

He leaned forward, brushing his lips lingeringly over hers. He felt her hesitation, her initial resistance, then she placed her palm against his cheek and kissed him back, unleashing the powerful attraction he had for her. Attraction that was merely lust. Merely the need to make her his once more.

* * *

As Kaliana prepared for a night at the opera with Rafe she tried to maintain the demanding Princess act. She'd only been able to hide behind it for a while whilst trying on big bright diamonds which glittered like stars. Then she'd seen her ring. It had caught her attention. Teasing Rafe had been fun, but a large flashy ring wasn't her at all. She smiled at his stunned silence as she'd showed him the ring she wanted.

When she'd kissed him as part of the act, the shock which had zipped round her body made her realise how much she wanted him. She wanted him as much, if not more, than she had that first night. As if they really were already lovers. She was in danger of falling for him, becoming seduced by the passionate desire. Worse than that, she was in danger of handing over something equally as precious as her virginity. If she allowed herself to, she could easily hand this man her heart.

She was falling for him—not just the man she'd shared that amazing night with in London, but this man. She knew she shouldn't, but she couldn't help it.

She pushed back those traitorous thoughts, emerging from her room wearing a sapphire-blue full-length gown befitting the Princess she was. A zing of satisfaction rushed through her as Rafe looked up from his paperwork briefly, only to look back up a second time, his work forgotten. The plunging sweetheart neckline and diamanté-encrusted shoulder straps had got the reaction she wanted.

'You look…' He stood up from his desk, walking towards her, seeming to choose his words carefully. She'd never seen him lost for words.

'Good enough to convince your friend our engagement is real?' she finished for him, giving him a slow twirl to ensure he noticed the criss-cross diamanté straps across her bare back due to the low cut of the gown. She had no idea why, but she wanted to torment him, tease the desire they'd once shared back out into the open.

Slowly she turned, feeling his gaze on her. Feeling the burning of her skin as he watched her. Feeling the crackle in the air as the tension increased. Feeling in control. Just as she had been in the bar the first time they'd met. But had she really been in control?

The question made her pause briefly, but when she looked back up at him her breath nearly left her. The heavy desire in his eyes was too much, taking her back to the moment she'd looked into his eyes for the first time, knowing even then there was no going back. She'd known that her spontaneous rebellion to lose her virginity was going to happen. She'd wanted him then and she wanted him now with a carnal need she'd never known. Never believed possible.

That night in London she hadn't been in control; her desire had. Just as it was now.

She fought it. She couldn't allow it to take over.

'Beautiful,' he whispered. The air crackled as if fireworks were sparking around them. Kaliana held her breath. She couldn't move. Her heart was thudding.

Rafe moved towards her, that intoxicating darkness in his desire-laden eyes. 'Very beautiful.' His voice was thick and heavy. Her heart pounded with anticipation. Anticipation of his kiss. Only this time she didn't think she could turn it off, deny it, as she had done in the olive groves.

This time she wanted to stay. To taste his kiss and so much more.

'I have a role to play, that of a loving and willing fiancée.' Kaliana fought the sensation he'd set off inside her as he moved closer, but her words only intensified the desire in Rafe's eyes. She didn't think she could take such a hot sultry look from him for much longer and not act on it.

'A loving and willing fiancée?' Rafe repeated her words, following her lead.

She couldn't keep the sadness from her voice. 'Those were your terms to our deal, were they not? A deal born of duty.'

Once she and Rafe were married, all her father's problems would be over. She'd been so relieved to hear the worry had gone from her father's voice last week as they'd talked wedding details she'd almost forgotten the terms of the marriage she'd been forced to make.

Terms Rafe had dictated after kissing her so passionately in front of everyone.

She'd made a deal to marry a man so very dangerous to her naive and innocent heart. He could make her heart light, her tummy flutter with just a smile. Worse than that, he made her want to believe in something she'd thought impossible to find again. Love.

'Only duty?' Rafe's words cut through her like an unexpected bolt of thunder. 'What about desire? The powerful pull of attraction?'

She smiled brightly, trying not to read anything into his words. 'That is, of course, an added advantage.'

'*Sì, cara mia,* an added advantage, although this evening we need to portray romance and attraction. The desire can be saved for when we are alone, no?' He paused, looking down at her left hand, at the ring she'd chosen this afternoon. A small delicate stone she'd fallen in love with, but now that ring felt heavy. Like a lead weight dragging her down to the seabed as he continued to speak. 'Romance is something Franco and Francesca really believe in.'

'Is that a problem?' she asked tentatively. 'That the powerful businessman you are might believe in love?'

'On the contrary. Franco and Francesca believe we are in love, thanks to the press coverage of our whirlwind romance. It is something I wish them to continue believing.'

Kaliana's heart constricted, any faint hope that she might find a happy ever after with Rafe instantly slashed away. This man didn't want love. Didn't believe in it. For whatever reason, he had barricaded his heart away. It was all about his family wealth. His business. At least she was marrying to make the lives of her people better and not for her own personal gain.

'But you don't believe in love?' She knew he didn't. Knew the losses life had dealt him made that belief impossible, but for her own sanity she needed to hear him say it.

'No, I don't.'

'But you have loved once, Rafe?' As always, she couldn't help but probe deeper, needing to know more about this man. He'd already hinted at having lost his love and now she was unable to keep her curiosity under control.

'Once.' The answer was firm. It didn't invite further conversation, but she wasn't going to let this moment pass—a chance to find out more about him.

'Was it very long ago?'

'Almost ten years.' Rafe's expression changed, as if he was examining the past again. Guilt that she'd jolted obviously painful memories rushed through her. He looked at her. 'You know what it is like when you think you have found the person you want to spend the rest of your life with. You know how it hurts when that doesn't happen.'

She gasped, pressing her fingers to her lips. He'd lost his love to tragedy too?

'I'm sorry.' She walked to the large windows which gave an unrivalled view of the Trevi Fountain bathed in glorious sunshine and crowded by tourists all waiting to throw in a coin and make a wish.

'There is no need for sympathy. She simply decided her future wasn't with me.'

'It doesn't matter how you lose your first love; it still hurts,' she said softly, wanting to offer him some comfort but sensing that even a sympathetic tone would be unwelcome right now. He still loved her—his first love.

'We have both been burned by love.' The admission lanced through the atmosphere in the room, robbing her of the ability to think. She couldn't even turn to face him.

'So it would seem,' she said softly, thinking of Alif, realising she had given little thought to him or their love affair since spending time with Rafe. Not that she'd allow Rafe to know that, when the relationship between them was based purely on lust.

She turned to face him, wanting to end this conversation. It was too intimate. Made her question too many things, not least how she felt about Rafe. She shouldn't have pushed him to reveal his hidden emotions, not when she was in danger of wanting to be part of them too.

Her fleeting and fanciful dreams of Rafe

being the man she could discover love with were getting to her. All she'd ever wanted was love and happiness—the same kind her parents had once shared. Could a man as closed-off as Rafe, so obviously damaged by past emotions, ever love?

No. She had to remember that. Guard her stirring heart. And, more importantly, she would harden her heart. Lock it away. Freeze it. Anything to stop it from falling for this man.

She would be strong. As impenetrable as Rafe. Showcase her acting ability to the full tonight. Because, with a clarity she'd only felt once before—that first night in London—she knew she was in grave danger of losing everything to this man. In danger of loving him.

The evening had been a great success. Kaliana had played her part well over their evening meal, talking weddings and romance with Franco and Francesca. She'd been so convincing, Rafe himself had almost believed it. Almost believed she wanted to marry him for no other reason than she loved him.

She'd looked so beautiful, shining vibrantly as they'd chatted with the other couple over dinner. He had hardly been able to keep his eyes from her all night. The softness of her skin had tempted him as she'd sat watching the opera performance, totally caught up in the magic of the moment. She'd been so enraptured by it all, by the emotion of the story being told, he wondered if she really was as cold and emotionless as he was. As she'd claimed.

Right now, he wasn't sure if he was that devoid of emotion. He was all over the place. Kaliana was making him feel things he didn't want to. Things that brought back memories of the past, of a time when he'd been happy. All this was swirling through his mind as he guided Kaliana, with his hand gently in the small of her back, from the Teatro Valle to his waiting car.

As they left the building the night sky around them lit up with flashes. Kaliana moved closer to him. Instantly he turned protector, wrapping his arm around her, drawing her closer still. His body reacted to the contact and instantly he realised his mistake.

Kaliana tensed against him, but the Princess she was took over. She smiled for the cameras, flirted with them, and with him. Posing for the photographs he knew would make headlines in tomorrow's papers.

'Now there will be no peace from them. Soon everyone will want to know about the desert Princess you are marrying.' The heated remark pierced through the cool interior of the chauffeur-driven car as they left the pack of photographers behind and headed back to his apartment. She blamed him for the press interest. Anger glittered in her eyes, making them spark with gold, but he couldn't be swayed by it. Couldn't allow it to affect him. Allow *her* to affect him.

'But nobody will be in any doubt our engagement is real.' He tried to control the rollercoaster of emotions he was suddenly on. A rollercoaster that was beginning to reveal the things he'd long since locked away. 'Or that we are in love.'

'You could have warned me,' she snapped

and looked out of the window as the city's streets passed by.

He shrugged when she looked back at him. 'Why? You handled it like a pro. It's part of our deal, is it not? And, more than anyone else, I want my brother, Enzo, to believe our marriage is real.'

'Well, he won't miss that when it hits the headlines tomorrow.' She frowned at him. 'Why is it so important he knows?'

He didn't want to tell her, but something inside him snapped. The barrier of resistance broke and the pain of losing his twin, slowly but surely, since his mother's death, flowed freely. Along with the need to talk about him. To confide in Kaliana.

'I haven't spoken to my brother for several years. At least not properly. Not as a brother.'

He could see again his brother's angry face as they'd stood beneath the shade of a line of tall slender cypress trees at Villa Casella. He'd accused Rafe of gloating over his possible marriage break-up, of wishing it would happen. They had slipped so far apart. Torn by their love for the same woman. But now

Rafe didn't want that bad feeling to continue, didn't want to force guilt on his brother. He wanted Enzo to believe he was happy, especially with their father so ill.

His father's diagnosis had made him want to reach out to his twin, to mend the bridge which was in complete danger of collapse. Emma would want that too and he wanted to make Emma happy.

'What was the argument between you about?' The sharpness in Kaliana's voice had lessened, luring him into opening up—just a little.

It was as if Enzo was standing there with him right now. The words he'd said that day, the day his world had fallen apart, had been so cold. He could still hear them.

'Emma loves *me,* Rafe. And I love her. We are getting married.'

Rafe had retaliated and the argument which had followed had been loud and heated. Since then they had avoided one another, which meant Rafe hadn't had to see Emma with Enzo, but if she was happy then he was too. And Enzo and Emma had been happy—until the devastating news that Enzo couldn't father children. Children Emma had wanted. Children the Casella family had needed.

It had also put the spotlight on Rafe. The spare heir. Losing Emma had nearly killed him, and he certainly didn't want the dubious honour of producing the next Casella generation. Another reason why Enzo probably hated him even more.

Rafe looked at Kaliana. She was an only child. Would she understand sibling rivalry? Understand what being a twin meant? 'We compete for everything. Always have done and Emma was no exception.'

'Everything?' she asked quietly, unlocking more memories. Moments from his and Enzo's past that had become the foundation for the cold indifference between them when they were apart and the heated exchanges whenever they came together.

The car hummed along the streets of Rome, the evening lights dancing around the interior. Being in the sanctuary of the car, surrounded by Kaliana's concern and interest, pushed Rafe further away from his defensive wall. Taking her with him. Allowing her in.

The danger of allowing Kaliana in outweighed the pain of those memories. The realisation that it shouldn't have been like that. He and Enzo were twins, but that had never meant anything to Enzo. 'At school it was grades. At home it was the attention or approval of our parents.' The echo of that constant need to please his father, to gain his respect, lingered painfully. Respect that Enzo had received so easily. Maybe that was why their mother had favoured Rafe. Or at least that was what Enzo had always claimed, always jealously taunted him with.

Rafe continued, lost in the past, 'Then as we grew older it was women, business deals.'

'It doesn't have to be that way, Rafe. You should send him an invitation to the engagement party—and the wedding.' He could see Kaliana's mind working. Could see the rush of questions going through her mind. If only she knew the truth. 'You could mend it. Get your brother back. Your twin.'

As they exited the car, Rafe inwardly

flinched. Kaliana had hit the target. He did want his brother back. The brother who'd played as a young boy at Pietra Bianca with him. The brother who'd had his back when they started school. But not the brother who'd turned against him, taking from him the woman he'd loved.

'I really think you should.' Kaliana pushed home her point, seeing the uncertainty in his expression as they entered the apartment. 'Our marriage is about securing our families and surely your brother won't want the Casella wealth to pass to a more distant relation. One who doesn't bear the Casella name.'

Target achieved. She felt the dart of her words strike its centre.

Rafe looked at her, as if seeing her for the first time. Or at least seeing her as an ally in the path they had both chosen together.

He moved closer to her. She held her breath as he stood looking down at her, so close now she only had to move forwards a little to step into his arms. To reach up and kiss him.

Gently, he brushed her hair back, using that

sexy smile he must know she couldn't help but react to. 'You are right.'

'I know I am.' She smiled, flicking her brows up in the way she had the first time they'd met. The bold woman she'd been that evening, the woman he'd made her, had pushed back all pretence of being a princess making a marriage of convenience. She was now a woman who knew what she wanted—Rafe.

He laughed, that soft sexy sound which melted her core, shattered her defensive barrier, allowing him in. Allowing him emotionally close. 'You are also quite the seductress.'

'But that's what you like about me, isn't it, Rafe?' she teased him, leaning closer, pressing her lips together, inviting his kiss. Challenging him to refuse.

She couldn't help herself. He did something to her. Changed her with just a smile. All she wanted now was a repeat of the last time they had been alone. The difference this time was that Rafe was the one trying to shut himself away, be someone he wasn't.

'Rafe?' she questioned gently, knowing

what would happen when he kissed her. Knowing the explosive chemistry between them would be too much to ignore. Knowing the desire which hummed through the very essence of her body was sparking between them. Knowing once she kissed him back, allowed the desire to take over, she would be lost. She was mad. Insane. But she wanted that madness. It made her feel alive. Real.

She wanted them both to feel the desire, to forget everything, lose themselves in the passion.

Rafe wrapped his arms around her, pulling her against him, the evidence of just how much he wanted her unmistakable. His dark eyes bored into hers and her heart pounded, echoing the beat of desire deep within her.

She brushed her lips over his then stepped back from him. Testing him. Teasing him. Slowly she reached out, taking his hand, gently pulling him away from the window. She didn't want to say anything. Didn't want to break the spell.

'Don't do this, Kaliana,' he said, his voice

rough and deep. Wild and feral. 'Not unless you want a repeat of London.'

'I want that, Rafe. Tonight, I want that.'

His kiss, hard and demanding, told her all she needed to know. He wanted it too. He wanted her. Right now, it didn't matter what outside influences had brought them together; all that mattered was this passion. This desire. This need for one another.

She kissed him back, allowing the passion she'd held back to flow freely. With a feral growl full of hungry desire, he swept her from her feet, carrying her to the bed. He laid her on it, standing over her as he pulled his bow tie undone, his eyes never leaving hers.

'*Dio mio*, I can't help myself.' He tossed the tie aside, hastily opening his shirt buttons.

She smiled up at him, loving the power of this moment. The power she had over him. She sat up, grabbed at his open shirt, pulling him closer, forcing his body onto her as she lay back on the bed. She was going to take this moment, this night, and lose herself in it. Lose herself in the lovers' game. 'Then don't.'

CHAPTER SEVEN

THE EARLY SEPTEMBER heat in Sicily did little to calm the scorching memories of the week Kaliana had just spent with Rafe in Rome. For one whole week they'd spent every night together and, much as she'd tried not to, Kaliana knew that each time they'd made love she'd become a little closer to Rafe. By day they had held hands as they'd explored the city and it had felt so much more than just an act. At night the explosive passion had backed that up and Kaliana had begun to open her heart to him.

She looked at Rafe as he joined her in the large open-plan living room of Villa Casella after having talked with his father. He took her breath away. His tall, athletic body she knew so well, dressed in a dark suit which emphasised his masculinity to perfection.

His sex appeal. As he crossed the room and poured them both a glass of red wine, she couldn't take her eyes off him. She was falling harder for him every day.

How had she let that happen? How had he slipped beneath the barriers she'd erected around her heart to keep Alif in and other men out? She hadn't wanted to feel anything for another man, believing it would be almost as bad as adultery. Why wasn't she doing anything to stop herself falling in love with Rafe?

Her love for Alif was dimming, and it felt both liberating and sad.

Would Alif really have denied her love and happiness? He'd been such a kind and caring man. So eager to please her that he'd agreed to not having sex until they were married. She'd saved herself for Alif, but fate had changed that. Changed her.

Rafe handed her the glass of wine, drawing her from her melancholy thoughts, a sexy smile on his lips, that desire-laden darkness in his eyes. She knew that Alif would never have begrudged her happiness. Even if that meant loving another man. He would have been the first person to tell her to go out there and live her life. Find love again.

So why couldn't she? Even when it was so tantalisingly close to her.

You're scared of the pain. Pain that will come when the heat of attraction cools.

'You look beautiful tonight.' Rafe's eyes devoured her, making her body tingle with need. Heat unfurled within her as she recalled how often they'd made love in Rome. The first night had been so hot. So wild. She'd slept entwined in his arms, blissfully happy. That slumber had been invaded by yet more desire and in a sleepy haze he'd made love to her again, but that time it had felt so different, so intimate. She'd felt the heat of him as he'd entered her, skin against skin, and the freedom of that had pushed her over the edge, instantly dragging him with her, blocking out the reality of what was happening. The consequences which could follow. Something she now increasingly worried about.

'Thank you,' she said softly, taking a sip of the velvety red wine. She pushed that worry aside. After all, they would soon be married. She lowered her lashes as the hot memory of that moment of pure, unadulterated freedom fired desire through her once more.

'If you continue to look at me like that, I'll be forced to take you to my room—right now.' He moved a little closer, the spark of sexual energy jumping wildly between them.

She raised her brows at him, feeling like the woman who'd walked into that bar the first night she'd met him. The woman who'd wanted to cast off all her inhibitions along with her past, and be his for that night. She loved the freedom that memory gave her.

'That would be wholly inappropriate, Raffaele Casella,' she taunted, looking at him as she tasted the berries and the sunshine that had made the wine. 'Your father has allocated us separate rooms, for propriety. And it's something my father will also expect to see in place when he and my mother arrive.'

'Maybe.' He smiled and sipped his wine.

'How is your father today? Will he be well enough to attend the party tomorrow?' Kaliana needed to change the subject, needed to keep herself focused on what was really going on. She couldn't allow the passion, the ever-deepening emotions she felt for Rafe, to cloud the reality of the situation. The cold, practical deal they'd made to marry and have children.

Whatever she did, she had to tell herself that the desire between them was just lust. No matter how much she now secretly yearned for it, that lust could never be love. She had to remember what he'd told her. Like her, he'd loved and lost.

'He is responding well to his treatment, although it is taking it out of him physically.' Rafe stepped back from her. From the spark of sexual energy. 'Our engagement party has given him a new surge of life. He is determined to be well enough to celebrate with everyone.'

The reminder of what tomorrow would bring made her tense. A high society party here, at Villa Casella, to seal the deal she'd made with Rafe. The marriage deal made purely for convenience. Tomorrow, she and Rafe would officially be engaged.

Photographers from *Vive*, Italy's top celebrity magazine, were due to arrive in the morning. The fact that her engagement photos would be seen around the world was daunting enough. But, worse than that, tonight, among the many guests due to arrive, from Franco to Claire, was Enzo.

Kaliana had hoped he would come, hoped that this would be the beginning of the brothers—the twins—creating a new friendship. Rebuilding their relationship. 'It will be nice for him to see Enzo, to have both his sons together.'

'Enzo and I have agreed to put our differences aside,' Rafe said, his shoulders tensing. 'We've agreed to do that because our father is ill. Because he needs to believe we are now united. That together we will ensure the Casella inheritance remains just that. It doesn't mean I have forgiven him for anything.'

'Sometimes you have to let go of things from the past and move on, even if you don't feel good about it.' The words rushed from her and, looking at Rafe, she wondered why she'd said that. Was she trying to help heal wounds between him and Enzo? Trying to make him move on from the loss of his first love? Or was it because she was beginning to feel ready to do just that herself? That she was looking for her own approval.

Rafe looked at her, the hardness of his gaze leaving her in no doubt that her outburst had doused the flames of desire which had been whipping around them just moments ago. Maybe that was for the best.

'Enzo and I have…' he paused as if searching for the right words '…a very complicated past. One that can't just be put aside.'

'You can act like my lover, act as if we are in the middle of a whirlwind romance, for the sake of your family, so maybe, for the sake of your father, you and Enzo can not only portray the image of twins who have forgiven and forgotten, but actually do that. Actually forgive one another.'

Rafe looked away, as if ashamed of his thoughts. 'I'm not sure I can ever forgive or forget what Enzo did. He took Emma from me.'

'And you loved her?' Kaliana stepped forward, sensing Rafe's pain, wanting to help him heal as she was beginning to heal.

He looked up at her, questions and doubt in his eyes where desire had only recently been. 'I can't do this now, Kaliana. I know you mean well, that you think we should mend the broken bridges between us, but it takes two to do that.'

'If Enzo comes tonight?' She asked the question softly.

'Then maybe we can start to rebuild those bridges. But it will take time. And trust. On both sides.'

Had the argument between the twin brothers blown up because Enzo, the eldest, had discovered he was unable to father children? Because he couldn't do the one thing his father expected of him? Or did it go back much further? To Emma? All sorts of questions rushed through Kaliana's mind and she wished Rafe didn't shut her out so much. Wished he'd let her in.

But that would be more like being real lovers. And they weren't. They were acting the roles of lovers. For their own gains. Why did just being with Rafe cloud that sentiment? Make her wish for more?

'Franco and Claire are due to arrive soon.' Rafe's words interrupted her thoughts, bringing her back to reality at a startling speed. He'd clearly put their conversation to one side, focusing instead on what they needed to do as a couple. She wondered if Franco knew the truth of the arrangement, as Claire did. Somehow the idea of Rafe confiding in anyone, even his lifelong friend, didn't seem possible.

'I'm looking forward to seeing Claire,' she said, attempting to put some distance between the feelings deep inside her and the reality in front of her. 'It will be good to catch up.'

'It will be nice to dine with Franco and Francesca as well as Claire, no?' His voice now held that seductive amusement she found so hard to resist.

She loved the way he added no to the end of his questions. As if he doubted she could ever agree with him. It was just one of the many things about Rafe she'd grown fond of during their time in Rome.

'It will be really nice for Claire and Franco to meet and get to know one another.' Kaliana smiled up at him, revelling in the gentle closeness surrounding them—as if he cared, even though he'd actively shut her out emotionally once more. 'After all, they will be best man and bridesmaid.'

'*Sì,* it will be a good thing. And Franco tells me Francesca is excited to see you again,' Rafe said, that hint of amusement lingering in his voice.

'I don't think she believes it's possible the most untameable bachelor is getting married,' Kaliana teased him. She couldn't help herself.

'Is that what I am?' He moved closer to her again, the coldness of their discussion about Enzo seemingly forgotten.

'Didn't you know that?' She laughed. 'The headlines after our night out in Rome said that a mysterious princess had tamed the world's most untameable bachelor.'

'Mysterious.' He moved closer. 'I like that.'

'And being tamed?' she teased him again, unable to help herself. Especially when she knew that next he would brush his lips over hers in a sexy and very teasing kiss.

As if he read her thoughts, he smiled then lowered his head, brushing his lips over hers. 'It's a pity we are to be apart tonight, no?' he whispered against her lips. She laughed softly, like a teenager who'd finally got to go out with her crush.

'So the rumours are true.' A new voice broke into the sensuality of the moment. Kaliana sprang back from Rafe, turning to see a man who could only be Enzo. Inwardly she sighed with relief. He'd come. There was hope of making things right. That had to happen. Deep down she knew that whatever was going on between these two was linked to Rafe's impenetrable barriers.

She watched him as he walked into the room, as tall and as powerfully commanding as Rafe, but there was a hard edge to his expression. The hope that Rafe and his twin could mend things faded slightly.

'By that, I assume you mean that my fiancée and I are very much in love?' Rafe's voice bristled with irritation. And something else. Warning.

'And there I was thinking you'd finally decided to do your family duty and marry for the good of the Casella name. To have the heir we all need.' Enzo's voice was cautious as he came to stand in front of them, looking at her.

She could hear his unspoken questions. This was the one person Rafe had wanted to believe the whirlwind romance story. But from the look on Enzo's face, Kaliana suspected he wasn't fooled. He knew it was a marriage deal to keep the family fortune. Something he was unable to do himself. She couldn't tell Rafe now, that maybe she already carried the heir they all required. It would have to wait until they were married. Until Rafe and Enzo had rebuilt their relationship.

'So, tell me...' Enzo directed the question at her, smiling, the same curve to his lips as Rafe. She forced her thoughts back. Focused on the moment. 'How did my brother persuade a princess to become entangled in the Casella family?'

'Enzo…' Rafe growled, moving closer to Kaliana, putting his arm around her, drawing her against him. Staking his claim on her.

That possessive action was because Enzo had stolen his first love, Kaliana reminded herself, nestling even closer to Rafe as the need to stand up for him—for them and what they were doing—surged forwards. 'It was one of those instant attraction moments,' she said quickly, trying to deflect the tension which was weaving around them. Tightening its grip. 'And we haven't looked back since, have we, Rafe?'

Rafe's arm tensed around her and her heart began to race. 'No, we haven't.'

Enzo turned his full attention onto her. That expression of doubt she'd seen so many times before tugged at her guilty heart. He had the same seductive and very sexy smile that Rafe had. It made her pulse leap. Not with attraction, as with Rafe that very first night in London, but with her own loss and fear. She shouldn't allow it, but the worry of consequences from that night in Rome was seeping ever deeper.

Shock was the motivator for that pounding in her head. Shock that right now, right here, in front of his twin, the brother he'd already lured a woman away from, Enzo was once again turning on the charm. Was he really trying to seduce her away from Rafe—his own brother? Or was it to make a point? To prove that he knew the love between them wasn't real. Was he testing her?

Enzo must know they were acting. That it was all role play. He was trying to seduce the truth from her.

'That's very convenient,' Enzo said, his brows flicking upwards suggestively.

'Enough.' Rafe's voice was steady. Hard. Enzo turned his attention to his brother as Rafe continued. 'Kaliana is my fiancée, the woman I will be making my wife, and you will show her some respect.'

The hot sultry evening air froze around them. The crackle of ice hardening, filling the air, was laden with gut-wrenching tension.

Enzo turned to Kaliana. 'My sincere apologies.'

Before she could see what was coming, Enzo moved towards her, the customary kiss on each cheek planted on her. It was like being in a tug-of-war—Rafe rigidly holding her close, keeping his arm around her, Enzo following the expected protocol. Kaliana knew for sure he was exploiting it to goad Rafe.

'Apologies accepted.' She pulled back.

Voices in the hallway alerted Kaliana to Claire's arrival and when her friend walked in, accompanied by the tall and distinguished Franco, with Francesca looking so elegant that Kaliana wanted to rush off and change her emerald-green dress, she breathed a sigh of relief.

'Claire, thank goodness you are here.' She all but dragged her friend into the room, relief bursting through her. Finally, she could talk to someone about the confusion of emotions pounding through her.

'Problems?' Claire whispered as she glanced at Rafe and Enzo, now greeting Franco and Francesca.

'It's probably just me. I'm really nervous,'

Kaliana said quietly, keeping the smile pinned to her lips as she felt Enzo's scrutiny on her once again. She couldn't say anything here. Not yet. 'Who wouldn't be nervous? I'm engaged. And very soon I'll be married.'

Claire took her hand, squeezing it reassuringly, and Kaliana relaxed. Claire understood and, more importantly, she was here for her. A friend she could rely on. A friend she could trust. Even with her worst fear.

'I think I may be pregnant,' she whispered.

Claire laughed softly, rubbing Kaliana's arm. 'Does it really matter now if you are?'

Rafe watched Kaliana as she spoke to Claire, the women's friendship and support clear. Guilt rushed through him. He should have backed Kaliana up. Should have told Enzo he and Kaliana were in love. Instead he'd remained silent while she'd stood up to Enzo. He'd allowed the past to rear its head again. He turned his attention to Enzo and Franco, the flurry of Italian now flowing between them as Francesca listened intently. He needed to get Enzo alone, needed to discuss things privately with him.

'Marriage will suit you,' Franco said to Rafe, drawing him from his thoughts. His friend smiled warmly at Francesca as he wrapped her close to him, the love between the couple as clear as the sparkling sea surrounding Sicily. The kind of love he'd thought he'd had with Emma, before Enzo had taken her from him. Could he have got that so wrong?

'Kaliana is very beautiful.' Francesca smiled, looking across the room to where Claire and Kaliana were deep in conversation. With her emerald-green dress hugging her slender figure, she looked the picture of elegance. Regal elegance. Every inch the Princess.

'She is, yes,' Rafe agreed. 'She is beautiful—inside and out.'

Watching Kaliana, he realised she was exactly that. But more startling was the realisation that she was so like his mother— a woman with strength and compassion in equal measures. The kind of woman his mother had urged him to find. The kind of woman who didn't deserve to be trapped in a loveless marriage. A woman who deserved to be loved.

Kaliana was everything he needed to put the hurt behind him without tarnishing the memories of happier days by dragging the past into the present.

So why couldn't he let her in?

Why did he want to push her as far away as possible emotionally?

'I see she's already got to you,' Franco said, his voice full of amusement. Then his expression turned more serious as Enzo was greeted by another guest, becoming embroiled in conversation. 'Don't shut her out, Rafe. It may be a marriage of convenience, but she is just what you need.'

Instantly Rafe was on his guard. 'I don't understand what you're talking about.'

Franco knew. He knew their romance wasn't real. Rafe couldn't have this conversation. He couldn't have this manly heart-to-heart right here, right now. He glanced at Kaliana, at the way the soft evening light glowed in her hair as she stood by the windows opening onto the terrace, her face filled with pleasure and happiness as she and Claire talked and laughed.

Last night, and every other night in Rome, her face had shone with pleasure and desire—desire they'd shared. But could he give her what she really deserved? Could he give happiness? Love?

Kaliana deserved happiness. She was giving up so much to save her small kingdom from financial shame, prevent her people living in poverty. Just like his mother, she had a loving and giving heart. Exactly the kind of woman he should love. But he couldn't. Not until he'd drawn a line under the past. A big bold line.

Yet still he was drawn to Kaliana. She was taking him back to a place he'd never wanted to go again. A place where his emotions would be exposed. A place where those emotions would be so very vulnerable. He couldn't allow that. He couldn't go there again.

'I've seen the way you look at her.' Franco said. Rafe snapped his attention back to his lifelong friend. The only person outside his family who knew everything, who knew all the pain he'd endured. He was the only man who knew why he'd barricaded his heart.

'You have seen through our façade. And yes, I do like for her, but convenience is the only reason we are marrying,' Rafe said after ensuring Enzo was out of earshot. 'What you think you see is just the charade of being lovers.'

'And you, my friend, forget I know you as well as you do. Maybe even better than you know yourself.' Franco placed his hand on his shoulder, a knowing smile on his face.

'Now you are talking nonsense,' Rafe said, unnerved by the way Franco went straight to the core of his fears. The reason why Rafe had to ensure that the sizzling attraction between him and Kaliana remained at the forefront of the relationship. That attraction, that sexual chemistry, had to remain his reason for agreeing to their deal as much as fulfilling his duty. Nothing else could ever become the reason.

'Hi.'

Kaliana's voice, as she and Claire joined them, jolted Rafe from his traitorous thoughts.

'This is Kaliana's friend Claire, and this is Franco and his lovely wife, Francesca.' Rafe made the introductions, aware of Claire watching him. He could feel her disapproval. Her doubt. Was he to be cross-examined by both Franco and Claire?

Francesca moved towards Kaliana, kissing her warmly on both cheeks. 'It's so lovely to see you again and be here to celebrate your engagement.' She then embraced Claire in the same way, with the same warm welcome. 'And to meet you, Claire.'

Kaliana had found it difficult to relax as the formal meal started. The small group had enjoyed lively conversation but, by unspoken agreement, nobody had mentioned their engagement, or the impending wedding.

That, together with her ever-increasing worry, had been so overwhelming that she hadn't been able to face going into her room alone after everyone else had retired for the night. Instead she slipped out into the peace and quiet offered by the villa's terraces. The velvety black sky cloaking everything in softness, soothing the ache in her heart.

She inhaled a deep breath of the warm scented air, hugging her arms about her. The sounds of the night calmed her. She rubbed her hands up and down her arms, slowly beginning to relax.

The time she'd spent in Rome with Rafe had been like living in a bubble. A bubble of passion and happiness. A bubble where she'd begun to dream, begun to wish and want for more. Now the reality of what their engagement would mean, and their wedding, began to banish that relaxed state she'd managed to find.

'Couldn't sleep without me?' Rafe's teasing words startled her and she whirled round to face him. He'd discarded his jacket and the white of his shirt was stark and bright in the darkness of the terrace. The array of foliage growing up the trellis as shade against the sun shrouded him in darkness, making him seem more unreachable than ever.

'Something like that,' she said softly, the

warm breeze feeling like a caress on her face, reminding her of Rafe's touch. How it felt. How it made her dare to hope. 'It's hard to believe this is really going to happen. That we are going to be married.'

He walked towards her, coming out of the shadows, and she could see the concern on his handsome face. Feel it with every nerve in her body. It made her breath hitch, her heart race. It was as if he cared. Really cared. Like a lover would.

'It is what you want?' Rafe touched her arms, gently turning her to face him, the concern in his expression so clear, despite his face still being partially shrouded in darkness.

'It's what I have to do, Rafe.' She spoke softly, reservations coursing through her. Regret even. 'Marriage is what I have to do. If not to you, then to Nassif.'

A look of regret crossed Rafe's face that even the darkness of the terrace couldn't hide. Was he wishing he hadn't agreed to their marriage deal?

'You are doing a very honourable thing.'

Rafe reached out, brushing her hair from her face. 'Giving up your chance of happiness and love for the sake of your country, your people.'

'It is expected of me, Rafe.' A horrendous thought rushed through her mind. What was he trying to tell her? 'You are having second thoughts, aren't you? You don't want this any more?'

All sorts of scenarios assailed her. Her father's disappointment. The shame she would bring to her family—to the country—if she didn't marry. Because how could she if she carried Rafe's child? The people of Ardu Safra would be forced to live under strict austerity if the country financially collapsed. Or, worse, if her father was forced to step down, unable to solve the issues he'd kept hidden from her for the last five years. What would happen to the country then? To her people? Her family?

It was unthinkable. As unthinkable as the possibility that she might be pregnant. Because if Rafe was having second thoughts...

'No, I am not having second thoughts.' His

soft words dragged her back from the fearful thoughts. 'Like you, this is something I have to do. Marriage is my duty.'

His answer hurt, his honesty cutting to the core. But what would she have done if he'd said something else? If he'd told her he wanted to marry her because he loved and wanted her? It was unsettling to even think of acknowledging this was what she'd secretly hoped for.

'It's always been that way, Rafe.' She couldn't allow him to derail her now. This marriage had to go ahead. For her country's sake—and for hers. Even if she wasn't pregnant, she could not, would not, marry Nassif. 'And once all the requirements of the marriage have been met, we can go our separate ways, live our own lives.'

He smiled at her. Like a lover might. Like he'd done in London that first night and all those nights in Rome. 'It will take some time to meet all the requirements, no?'

She pressed her eyes closed, hoping he couldn't see her face in the dark. Hoping he wouldn't notice her despair.

'Is it so bad, *cara*?' He spoke softly, gently lifting her chin, giving her little choice but to look up at him. She opened her eyes. Saw that all too familiar desire in his. 'When we have something so good?'

'No,' she whispered, feeling herself drawn to him, being lured closer, like a bee to a newly opened flower. She wanted him. Wanted him to want her. 'No, it isn't.'

He pressed his lips to her forehead and, closing her eyes, she inhaled deeply, trembling with need. And something more. Something far more dangerous to her heart.

'Rafe...' she whispered. Unable to understand the emotion filling her right now. One she couldn't bear to name.

She opened her eyes, pulling back to look up at him. Desire filled his eyes.

'I don't want to let you go tonight,' he whispered, the soft evening breeze turning those words into a caress. Or was that her wishful thinking?

'We have to be apart,' she said, desperate to prevent her words becoming a husky whisper.

'Here, and again when we are in Ardu Safra, before the marriage ceremony.'

'Are you saying I cannot make love to you until our wedding night?'

She smiled up at him, revelling in the knowledge that he wanted her. It gave hope. Stirred those emotions she couldn't admit to. 'Yes,' she whispered.

'But you don't want that, do you, *cara mia*?' He was teasing her again.

'No, I don't.' Boldly she made her claim, looking at him from beneath lowered lashes. 'But it's what we must do. We are marrying for tradition and we must uphold that tradition.'

'That is Princess Kaliana talking,' he said firmly, his eyes sparking with desire and laughter.

'Kaliana will have to wait her turn.' She laughed.

'Then I will say goodnight.' He gently drew her closer and Kaliana moved willingly against him, feeling every hard contour of his body. A body she knew and loved so much.

'She will be back,' she whispered against

his lips, unable to help herself, as he lowered his head to kiss her. 'But not until we are married.'

The light teasing touch of his lips became hard. Demanding. Instantly her body was alight. Needing his. His hands splayed out across her back, keeping her body close against his, leaving her in no doubt as to how much he wanted her. His other palm skimmed down her side, his fingers brushing briefly against her breasts, making her sigh into his kiss.

'Can she wait that long?' he whispered, his forehead pressed against hers.

Her body was pounding with need. Screaming with desire. She couldn't give into either. If she did, she'd be opening the doors to the feelings she hadn't wanted. Emotions she'd thought she'd never feel again. Emotions she knew he wouldn't—couldn't—ever feel.

'She can.' She almost gasped out loud as he kissed her neck. Damn him, he already knew just where to kiss her. And how. 'And she will.'

'Spoilsport,' he said as he stepped back

from her, his breathing deep and as uncontrolled as hers.

'Our deal has to come first, Rafe.' She dragged the Princess to the fore. Hauling out all the reasons they were marrying as defence against the one thing she didn't want to feel again.

He nodded slowly, seeming back in control of himself. 'You are right.' He held out his hand to her. 'Shall we retire to our very separate rooms?'

Kaliana took his hand. Princess Kaliana would have flounced past him, but she couldn't. He was offering her one tiny bit of romance, one small gesture of caring. And she, Kaliana, needed that almost as much as she needed him.

CHAPTER EIGHT

RAFE HAD ENDURED a restless night after he had escorted Kaliana to her room. He'd lain awake for hours, his body craving hers, but it was the expression on her face, the softness in her eyes hinting at so much more, which haunted him.

As that softness, the same loving glow Emma had once had in her eyes for him, had burned brighter, he'd inwardly panicked. Was it possible that Kaliana felt something for him? That she could be falling in love with him? He didn't want or deserve her love.

The startling revelation had rocketed through him and he'd watched her slam down the shutters on her emotions. He'd seen the moment she stopped being Kaliana, the woman he'd met that first night in London, and become Princess Kaliana, the woman he

was marrying. A marriage for duty and tradition. For both of them.

Now, on the evening of their engagement
party, he waited at the bottom of the grand
staircase in Villa Casella. As of this evening
they were officially engaged, their wedding
just weeks away. For both of them, their lives
would change once they were married.

He waited, his heart thudding. Who would
come and stand at the top of the stairs and
look down at him? The woman he'd first met?
The fiery passionate woman whose virginity
he'd taken? Or the cool and aloof Princess,
bound by duty to do what was necessary? He
wanted—no, needed—the emotionless and
practical Princess. He didn't want to have to
look into the eyes of the woman who'd strode
into the bar that night in London. The night
he'd been drowning his sorrows over the marriage he had been forced to make. The night
she had been looking for something—someone—to take her mind off her problems.

Above him a door clicked open, and then
shut. He clenched his teeth, biting down hard.
She had to be the Princess. If he saw any soft-

ness on her face, any hint of what he'd seen so briefly last night, he wouldn't be able to go through with this at all. He looked upwards, the intricate wrought iron balustrades allowing him to see who was on the landing.

Red silk of a long dress was all he could see at first as she moved to the top of the stairs. Rafe slowly lifted his eyes, looking up to the figure of the woman who'd ignited such passion in him he was in danger of forgetting himself. Forgetting what he needed to do.

As he looked into her eyes, she remained still, looking down at him. He could feel those gold-flecked eyes of hers taking in every detail. Was she too fighting the urge to turn her back on her duty, her family?

His gaze met hers. Showering over him like the first flurry of snow in winter. Soft, yet bitterly cold. The eyes of Princess Kaliana. She stood defiantly at the top of the stairs, dressed in the most stunning red strapless ball gown. She looked…amazing. Every inch the Princess that she was. The Princess he needed her to be.

Behind him he heard gasps, then Franco's

soft chiding as he guided his wife away. 'Let's leave the lovers in peace.'

Rafe smiled at his friend's far from subtle comment. He and Kaliana might well be lovers, passionate lovers, but they were not *in love*.

Or at least that was what he'd thought— until last night.

Rafe moved to the bottom step, holding out his hands as Kaliana came down. Regal elegance shone from her like the brightest star.

'So, this is it,' she whispered to him. 'The moment everything becomes official.'

Rafe smiled. 'Very official. Especially when you wear these.'

He'd been holding the box containing the priceless Casella necklace, earrings and bracelet so tightly he almost couldn't move his arm, couldn't show her the box. His movement was far from fluid as he opened the box, holding it out to her.

'I wasn't expecting this.' Her gorgeous eyes were wide with shock and beneath her polished exterior he'd glimpsed the Kaliana he really wanted. The Kaliana he couldn't have. Didn't deserve.

'The Casella jewels.' He forced the words out, pushing back those useless sentiments. 'And as the next Casella bride you will be expected to wear them tonight.'

Once he'd dreamt of giving them to Emma. Then she'd left him for Enzo. They had run away to marry in guilty secret, shunning that tradition.

'I can't wear these.' She reached out to touch them, proving that, like most women, she could be won over by the sparkle of a diamond or two.

'They are yours to wear today, our official engagement, and on our wedding day.'

He could see the question in her eyes. Hear her asking if Enzo had given them to his bride too. 'My mother was the last Casella bride to wear them. Enzo chose to marry in secret, so deprived his bride of that honour.'

As the explanation surged forward, Rafe realised he was happy it had happened that way. And that at least Enzo had had the decency to be guilty about all he'd done, running away with the woman his twin brother loved. In a rush of something he'd never taken the time to consider before, Rafe realised that Enzo had taken Emma away and married her because he was ashamed of what he'd done to his own brother.

'I see,' she said, her voice stern. 'In that case, can you…?' She gestured to the box in his hand, the unfinished question hanging between them.

He looked at her. At the bright gold flecks in her eyes now sparkling like angry fireworks. '*Sì, cara*, I can.'

He turned, laying the box on the hall table, taking out the heavy diamond necklace. He opened the clasp and looked at her, his eyes holding her gaze. Deep in those gold-flecked depths he saw fear. As if she was sacrificing herself.

Without a word she turned her back to him and waited. He allowed himself the guilty luxury of studying her naked shoulders before moving forward, encircling her body with his arms and the necklace, so that he could place it at her throat. She tensed as he fastened it. As his fingers brushed her skin her head bowed and she placed her palm over the gems.

Her breathing had become deeper and he fought the urge to turn her in his arms, to tell her it didn't have to be this way. To tell her it didn't have to be all about duty. That together they could both move forward. Slowly they could both regain their shattered belief in love.

What the hell was he thinking?

'Very beautiful,' she whispered as she turned to him, removing one of her small diamond studs in readiness to replace it with the matching earrings from the set. 'I had better wear it all, enter fully into the tradition, yes?'

'It will be expected of you.' He reached out, picking up one earring, its weight immense. And he was handing that weight of duty to Kaliana. The woman he could love, if only he had time to heal. If only she too could heal.

He watched as she put the earring in place then passed the second one, the weight of it more noticeable—the weight of his duty. His family duty.

She fastened the earring and picked up the bracelet, her arm brushing against him as she leant forward. 'Last one.' She smiled up at him. A smile which didn't quite reach her eyes. Did she sense the weight of those jewels, sparkling against her skin?

Kaliana could scarcely breathe. Rafe's fingers lingered on her skin, sending a flurry of hot desire-filled sparks through her. But, beneath her fingertips, the coldness of the jewels sealed their deal.

She would be a Casella bride. A deal to secure the future of the ancient Sicilian name with an heir. He was to be her husband, the man who saved her kingdom from financial ruin and her from a cruel loveless marriage.

She should be pleased. Relieved. It was going to happen. So why did she feel so disappointed? Why did she want more than that?

'They are very beautiful. I'm honoured to wear them.' The lie slipped with ease from the mouth of a princess trained from an early age how to be cool and calm. Unaffected. The Princess she now had to be if she stood any chance of holding onto her sanity in front of her parents and every other guest.

'As are you, *cara mia*.' Rafe's words were like a caress, the hungry look in his eyes as he looked at her real. She had to remember he performed the act of being in love almost to perfection. She couldn't forget what he'd told her. That love didn't have a place in his life.

She couldn't allow herself to weaken. Her heart was in danger of really falling in love with him.

He brushed her cheek with the backs of his fingers. 'Don't look so worried. Everything is going well. Even Enzo believes we are in love.'

'Enzo?' she questioned, the weight of those jewels increasing as all he'd told her about his mother being the last bride to wear them raced through her mind once more. Wouldn't her wearing them cause more upset between the two brothers? Discord she wanted to end.

'Will my wearing these cause more problems between you and your twin?' She couldn't hold the question back. Couldn't help but try to mend things. 'You should find a way to make it right between you and Enzo. I'm sure your father wouldn't want it, and your mother...'

She couldn't stem the flow of words. Couldn't stop herself from trying to help him. If she'd had a brother or sister, she wouldn't want animosity between them, simmering away.

'He may not be pleased, but he and his wife chose to slip away and marry in secret—his bride had no right to wear these jewels.' Rafe cut across her.

'I'm sorry, Rafe.' She moved closer, placing her hand on his chest, feeling the soft material of his tuxedo. 'It must be hard to lose your brother like that, especially now the problems he's had in his marriage have affected your life.' If she kept these things at the forefront of her mind, she'd remember why he was doing this. Why he was marrying her. She had to remember that.

'Hard doesn't come close.' He sighed, then smiled. 'But none of this is about Enzo—or his wife. This is about us and right now we have guests to showcase our romance to.'

'Then let's go,' she said, pasting a bright smile on her face.

He took her hand. 'We make a great team, Kaliana.'

Her heart broke. The heart that loved Rafe.

His hand, wrapped around hers, was warm. Safe. Secure. She looked up at him as he walked just a pace ahead of her, taking her into the crowd of friends and family. As she followed, the truth hit her. Hard.

She was in love with him.

For her, this engagement, this impending marriage deal, had now become very real. It was now so much more than a deal. So much more than a fake romance to be acted out in front of their friends. Whatever the outcome of their nights in Rome, she was in love with him.

Rafe spoke first in Italian to those around them and she listened to his sexy voice, keeping a smile on her face when all she wanted to do was run and hide from the turmoil of her emotions. When he spoke again in English, talking to her parents, the realisation that she'd fallen in love with another man, putting

Alif in the past, surged forwards. It was nothing compared to the future she would now face, married to a man who couldn't love her as she loved him.

'*Congratulazioni.*' The cheers went up from the crowd and glasses were raised at them. She kept her mask of happiness on her face. Kept hold of Rafe's hand.

His fingers were clasped around hers firmly, the warmth on her skin a reminder of the heat of the passion they'd shared. But was that passion enough? Again, doubts surfaced, threatening to manifest themselves into something bigger. Something she wouldn't be able to ignore.

She had to remember their deal. Remember the real reason she'd come to Rafe, a man she'd shared just one night of passion with. It was because she couldn't face life as Nassif's wife—married to a man as cruel and cold as Alif had been gentle and warm.

That is why you are here now. She forced those words into her mind, looking up at Rafe as romantic music began to filter through the warm evening air, refusing to give more thought to her increasing worry.

Rafe smiled at her, his eyes alive with amusement. Had he sensed her turmoil? Somehow heard her inner reasoning? 'We will be expected to start the dancing, *cara*.'

His voice was warm. Deep and sexy. It helped her to remember why she'd asked him to marry her. Why she'd thought she could spend the rest of her life as this man's wife.

Passion. Hot, sultry passion.

'Then we had better dance.' She glanced at her father as the array of emotions rushing through her for this man, and this situation they were in, made her voice husky, almost a whisper.

Rafe looked at her, his expression questioning. Did he see her doubts? Sense her fears? She looked away at the gathered guests, all expectantly watching them.

He took her hand and led her onto the terrace, now a dance floor, lit by a multitude of twinkling fairy lights. It was far too romantic for the kind of deal they'd struck. Something more suited to a fairy tale romance.

He stopped in the middle of the dance floor, looking so handsome in his black tuxedo, freshly shaved and oozing sex appeal, that her heart stopped before thudding wildly.

If only this was real. If only the complete romantic aura of this moment was real. She wanted to be able to allow herself to love this man. Be loved by him.

He inhaled deeply as he gently held her, bringing her body against his. She closed her eyes, unable to resist melting against him. Unable to resist falling in love with him further.

'You smell so good,' he whispered against her ear. She squeezed her eyes tight shut, a ripple of pleasure slipping over her, like the gentlest wave on a summer day. 'Too good. I don't know if I can hold you close and not kiss you.'

She opened her eyes, a smile coming readily to her lips as she leant back a little, looking up at him. She wanted him to kiss her. Wanted to lose herself in the illusion of love.

'I want you to kiss me,' she whispered as

she moved towards him, bringing her lips so close to his.

'Then how can I say no?'

His lips met hers. Gentle and coaxing. Everything she was struggling to hide rushed forward as she kissed him back.

His palm against the small of her back pressed her against him, but she didn't need that encouragement as her body melted into his. Like wax around a flickering flame, she lost herself to him. To the romance of the moment. To the love for him intensifying with every smile, every caress and kiss.

His tongue invited hers to dance and she sighed with pleasure, accepting that invitation, kissing him deeper, harder. The rush of love hurtling through her made it impossible to remember they were in the middle of a dance floor, being watched by friends and family.

He broke the kiss, tenderly brushing her face with his fingers. 'Very convincing,' he whispered, his eyes as black as the velvety sky at midnight. 'Almost too real.'

'Would real be so bad?' she asked tentatively, her mind, her resolve softened by the moment.

'It's not what we agreed, Kaliana.' His voice became sterner, although still a whisper, even though his fingers continued to caress her face. 'It's not what either of us wanted—or needed.'

'Things can change.' She smiled up at him, then quickly looked down, a blush spreading over her face. She was lost in the romance, still warmed by the love flowing through her. Love for this man. A man who'd actively banished love from his life. His heart. More than anything she wanted to tell him she'd fallen in love with him.

His hold on her slipped. His hand dropped from her face and when she looked back up at him his gaze, his attention, wasn't on her.

Kaliana turned in his loosened hold to look in the direction his attention had been taken. He was watching a woman who'd just walked in and was now mingling with the crowd. Her pale blonde hair stood out amongst the other guests, making her appear lost. Alone.

'Emma…' Rafe breathed the name of the

woman he'd once loved and as she looked up at Rafe, then to the blonde, Kaliana knew anything she felt for him was futile. The way he'd said her name told its own story. He still loved Emma. And she was here. To see him?

As all she'd just witnessed, all she'd just realised, sank in, Rafe let her go, moving away from her far more than just physically. Stretching her emotions so taut that at any moment they'd snap with a painful sting.

'Excuse me.' He moved away, leaving her adrift on a sea of emotions she'd never wanted to sail again. Emotions which held pain as much as pleasure.

'Of course.' She stepped away from him. Hating the sensation of total abandonment. She blinked back the threat of tears, annoyed with herself. Annoyed she'd allowed emotion to influence her, to make her want more than she should have.

She turned her back on the image of Rafe striding towards the pretty blonde—the woman who'd held his heart all this time. Had she come to reclaim Rafe? To tell him she'd made a mistake? That she loved him?

Unable to help herself, she watched Rafe as he reached Emma. She didn't need to hear his voice to know his concern for the other woman.

'What's going on?' Claire's voice dragged her from her self-pity, the conclusions she couldn't help but jump to.

She watched as Rafe touched Emma's arm in that same caring gesture he'd used on her. 'She is the woman Rafe loves. The woman who broke his heart…' She didn't care who overheard. Hurt and rejection cascaded through her like water over the highest falls.

'What?' Claire asked and Kaliana sensed the protective anger in her friend's voice. 'He can't back out now. You'll have to…'

'Marry Nassif,' Kaliana finished for her, then frowned as Enzo joined Rafe and Emma. Kaliana wished she could hear what was being said. She could see Enzo's annoyance in the square set of his shoulders. Emma looked from one to the other, appeal in her expression. Then Rafe hugged Emma. A hug that held so much emotion it broke Kaliana's heart. The heart which had only just accepted it was full of love for the man she was to marry. The man who loved another woman.

'It looks like Enzo and Emma are getting back together.' Franco's accented tones made Kaliana blink. She turned to Rafe's friend as questions fired through her, followed by the tiniest glimmer of hope.

'Back together? Enzo and Emma?'

Franco frowned. 'They are married—separated, but…' He paused as if searching for the right word. Kaliana's mind raced wildly as she watched him. Waiting. 'Circumstances pushed them apart. Rafe has been working hard to engineer this meeting over the last few weeks, sure he can help mend their marriage.'

'Rafe has?' She could feel herself stuttering. Hated herself for it. No wonder there was so much tension between the two brothers. She looked at Franco again. But Rafe had engineered this meeting. What did that mean?

She turned her attention back to Rafe as he moved away from Emma, still looking lovingly down at her. Their gazes were locked, then he turned to Enzo, clasping him in a manly hug before turning and walking away from them both.

'You have to go to him,' Claire said, touching Kaliana's shoulder, pulling her from her stunned and frozen state of shock.

'I can't.' How could she go to him when she'd just seen the truth of the love he still had for Emma? His brother's wife. How could her newly fledged love ever mean more than that?

'Go to him,' Claire urged softly, compassion in her voice. 'Go to him, Kaliana. Tell him.'

Kaliana turned to her friend. 'Tell him what?' She couldn't say anything about the possibility that she might be pregnant. Not now. How could Claire expect her to?

'That you love him.'

Kaliana gasped.

'I know you don't want to admit it, but you have to, Kal. You have to grasp this chance of happiness. Forget your stupid deal. Forget everything else. Even what you told me earlier. Tell him how you feel.'

Claire's impassioned plea made Kaliana's

head spin. Were her feelings, the love she'd only just recognised herself, so obvious to others?

'She's right,' Franco said firmly, confirming her suspicion. 'You and Rafe have something. You both need to let go of the past. Embrace it.'

Kaliana looked at Rafe's retreating back as he left the party—their engagement party—heading for the sanctuary and privacy of the villa. Could she do this? Put her heart on the line? Admit she loved him when he clearly still loved another woman?

As the questions whirled in her mind, making her shiver with cold dread, she turned to see Emma and Enzo embrace. And then Enzo kissed her tenderly on the forehead. He loved his wife. Emma, the woman Rafe also loved.

'No,' Kaliana said, not caring what Franco knew. 'No, I don't love Rafe. We don't have anything. There is nothing between us other than a mutually beneficial marriage deal.'

Rafe stood in the darkness of his office. He'd wanted time. Space. He needed to think. His emotions were running riot inside him. As he'd held Kaliana, as he'd kissed her, he'd felt the overwhelming burn of love. The one thing he didn't want to feel.

Whenever he'd allowed that emotion into his life, his heart, it had always let him down. Always left him in pain.

First his mother. Then Emma. Even his father and brother, damn it. He'd loved them all. And each one of them had caused him pain. It was a story that had repeated itself too many times. Made him question who he was.

'Why didn't you tell me how much Emma still means to you?' Kaliana's gentle question roused him from his self-pity. He turned to see her standing in the doorway, illuminated by the light from the party beyond the darkness of the office he'd retreated to.

The halo of light gave her an unearthly appeal, but he ignored it, focusing instead on her question. 'Even you've got to agree that it's a messy love triangle.' He laughed, realising for the first time just how silly he'd been to try and hang onto Emma, to hang onto the hope that she still loved him.

What kind of fool was he?

'About as messy as the marriage triangle I'm hoping to avoid if I marry you.' Kaliana's voice was harder now. Full of power. Determination. The voice of a princess.

'If?' He remained in the shadow of darkness, while she stood in the glow of light. If he dared to open up to her, dared to tell her that what he'd begun to feel for her far surpassed anything he'd ever felt for Emma, then he could move into that warm light. Step out of the shadows of a life without love. But he couldn't. 'We have a deal.'

'Exactly,' she said seriously. 'We have a deal. A deal the Casella family needs. A deal my country needs. And our feelings are irrelevant.'

He pressed his lips together, inhaling deeply. 'Yes, we have a deal and, whatever happens, I won't back out, Kaliana. I'm a man of honour. A man of my word. A man who will do his duty.'

And that duty was to marry the woman who'd turned his life upside down that first night in London, opening his heart even then.

'Then we should go back out there and undo any damage your moment with Enzo's wife, followed by your disappearing act, has done to our act of a whirlwind romance.' Her sharp words cut him, forcing anything he felt for her into hiding. The Kaliana he'd met, the Kaliana he'd made love to with such passion had already left him.

'That is precisely what we should do, but...' He paused, on the verge of asking her what she really wanted out of the marriage. From him.

'But what, Rafe?' The slap of her question was as stinging as her palm would be across his face.

The way he felt about Emma had never come close to what he felt for this woman. Kaliana made him hopeful for impossible emotions, but the Princess before him was so cold. So distant. Why the hell did he think a woman who'd agreed to have his children in order to save her country from financial ruin could ever have any kind of feelings for him? What kind of fool had he been?

Could he really go through with it? Could

he marry simply for convenience when he knew all his mother had wanted was for him to find love and be happy?

'Do you want this deal? This marriage?' The question snapped from him. 'Because I can find a way out.'

'You know I do,' she implored as she moved forward a step. Forward into the darkness. His darkness.

'Why?' He had to hear her say it. Had to hear her cold words.

'Because I can't...' She walked closer, stumbling over her words, darkness enveloping them both. 'I can't marry Nassif. Not because he is older than me. Or cruel. But because I loved Alif, his nephew, the man I should have married.'

Did she still love Alif?

He still loved Emma.

Not in the way he'd once done. Not with passion and desire. He loved her as a friend. Nothing more. And he wanted Emma to be happy; that was why he'd set up the meeting with her and Enzo. He needed to let go of

Emma and heal the long-standing coldness between him and his twin.

He looked at Kaliana, at the shadows hiding the expressions on her face. She still mourned and loved her fiancé. Could he ever compete with that? Was he worthy of trying to claim her love? Could he ever forget the past and love her?

He shook his head in answer to that last question. 'If that is what you want, we should get back out there and continue this show of romance.' He held his hand out to her. She looked at it and for a moment he thought she wasn't going to take it.

'It won't be for much longer,' she said as her hand fitted loosely into his. 'Once we are married, we can live separate lives.'

'We can indeed.' Why was he saying that? He didn't want a life separate from Kaliana. She was his life. A life he couldn't have. Her icy-cold words had already made that clear.

'I am returning to Ardu Safra in the morning with my parents.' Her words were so casual, so light and free of any painful emotion that Rafe stopped to look at her, bringing her to a stop too. She looked into his eyes, the gold flecks of hers almost dimming to nothing. He'd done that to her.

'That isn't what we planned, and I have meetings tomorrow. I can't go with you.'

'I know,' she said, her chin lifting defiantly. 'You can follow me there once you are finished—if marriage to me is what you want.'

She was leaving him. The moment his heart had opened up, the moment he'd begun to think he could love again, and she was leaving him. 'Marriage is what I need, Kaliana. What my family needs. I am the only male heir able to create the next generation. I have to marry and have children. If there was any other way, I'd take it.'

She sighed softly. 'You just said you want a way out, so I only want you to come to Ardu Safra if you want me.' She looked down. 'If you want me to be your wife. The mother of your children.'

'What about your duty? Your country?' He couldn't believe she was doing this. It was almost as if she was saying goodbye.

'I will get married on my twenty-sixth birthday. My father has already seen to that.'

'You'll marry Nassif?'

She nodded, swallowing hard, as if unable to bring herself to agree to that. She pulled her hand free of his, stepping back away from him. 'An arranged marriage is bad enough, but to a man who is in love with another woman? I can't.' She shook her head. 'I'm sorry, Rafe, I have to go.'

Before he could answer. Before he could process everything she'd said, Kaliana turned and walked away. He watched the red silk of her dress as she disappeared upstairs. He should go to her. Tell her he wanted her. Needed her. So why the hell couldn't he?

CHAPTER NINE

THE HEAT OF Ardu Safra was suffocating. Kaliana stood by the open window, breathing in the warm air coming in off the golden dunes of the desert she loved so much, in a futile attempt to ease her discomfort.

For five days she'd relived that last conversation with Rafe. Her heart ached and her body was numb. She felt sick and each day Rafe's silence intensified those feelings. He'd allowed her to walk away the night of their engagement. He hadn't even tried to stop her She'd changed from her red gown, leaving it and the Casella jewels in her room, her heart breaking into so many pieces as she'd prepared to leave.

She hadn't said a word to her father or mother about breaking off the engagement, hoping that Rafe would come, that he'd honour their deal. They'd believed her claim that she wanted time to prepare for the wedding, but each day she'd woken with that heavy dread in her stomach. Deep down, she knew it was more than just dread. Knew it was because she carried Rafe's baby.

Claire's arrival earlier today had at least offered her some comfort, someone to talk to and confide in. She now faced the prospect of admitting to her father not only that the man she'd agreed to marry no longer wanted her, but that because of the baby she couldn't now marry Nassif. Or anyone.

An admission she couldn't make. Didn't want to make. Just as she couldn't yet face finding out for sure if she was pregnant.

Kaliana sighed, turning from the window. For the last hour she'd stood there, barely seeing the golden landscape of her homeland. Once the ability to do just that would have given her so much pleasure. She'd always loved the way the dunes changed as shadow or sunlight fell over them, making them seem alive. Leaving her birthplace to make a new life in London had been hard. Just as hard as finding her dreams shattered after Alif's death. But Rafe's silence was even harder to endure.

She should be about to start her life again in Ardu Safra, with her new dreams. Tender dreams—but they'd been shattered too. Obliterated. And along with them her chance to help her country, her people.

'That sounds like a sigh of defeat,' Claire said from behind her. She heard her friend put down the book she'd been lost in and cross the marble floor, joining her at the window.

'I guess I have to accept Rafe doesn't want to marry me any more,' she said as she listlessly walked into the room, her soft slippers scuffing on the marble floor. How could it hurt so much? How could she feel this rejected when all they'd ever had was an agreement to marry for no other reason than their families demanded it of them?

'Kaliana?' Claire questioned, a worried expression on her face. Kaliana didn't like the question in her friend's voice, or the way she was watching her. 'Before you do anything, before you give up on Rafe, you have to do a pregnancy test. You have to know for sure.'

Kaliana frowned. 'I can't. Even if I happened to have one to hand.'

For a moment Claire hesitated and Kaliana looked at her, sensing the worry, seeing the fear on her friend's face. They'd known each other for five years, since Kaliana had moved to London, but they knew so much about each other it felt like a lifetime. More than anything Kaliana trusted her. Thought of her as her sister.

'I do.' Claire got up and walked quickly to the chair in the corner of the room and grabbed her bag, producing a slim blue and white box, holding it out to Kaliana. 'I got one, knowing you wouldn't be able to easily get hold of one.'

With a sickening lurch of her stomach Kaliana looked at Claire, panic making any words impossible. Could it really be possible? She and Rafe had made love many times whilst they'd been in Rome. Each time he'd used the protection of a condom. He'd never failed to protect either of them—except that one time in the early hours of the morning.

That one time when they'd made love as sleep had tried to hang onto their exhausted bodies. The time when she'd finally accepted she felt something more than just lust for him.

She shook her head in denial. 'I can't be pregnant. We used contraception.' She thought of the way her stomach turned over each morning as she got out of bed, of the waves of nausea which washed over her during the day. Every day since she'd arrived in Ardu Safra. No. She couldn't be pregnant. She couldn't. 'It's just nerves. Worry.'

'Kaliana,' Claire almost snapped. 'You have to do this test.'

'It's just the worry of everything.' Kaliana hotly denied what Claire was saying, even though deep down she knew it was almost certainly true. And where did that leave her?

'Then do this test. Prove me wrong. Prove yourself wrong,' Claire challenged.

'Very well.' There was only one way to find out. Kaliana took the box from Claire with a weak smile.

Kaliana's hands shook as she opened the box. What if she was pregnant? The father a man who didn't want her any more. A man she'd stupidly fallen in love with despite his warnings. *His* warnings that he couldn't love her—or anyone.

'I can't look,' Kaliana said as she opened the bathroom door, returning to her room a short time later, the look of concern and compassion on Claire's face bringing a fresh wave of nausea over her. 'Whatever it says, it won't make any difference. Whatever it was Rafe and I had is over. Finished.'

'Oh, Kal,' Claire soothed as she took the test from her. Kaliana watched her friend's face as Claire looked down at the test, her heart pounding with anticipation. With fear.

The sound of an approaching helicopter above the palace snatched Kaliana's attention from Claire, from the test. She hated those machines now. Hated that they'd taken away the man she'd loved. The man she should have married. Had her father sent for Nassif? Had he sensed there were problems? Had Rafe officially called it all off?

There was no way she could marry Nassif now. Not just because of the possibility that she carried Rafe's child, but because she loved him. Every limb ached with need for him. For his touch, his kiss. For his love.

Claire's silence suddenly seemed deafening, snatching her back from the thoughts of what love really felt like. She looked at Claire, her head lowered as she held the test in front of her.

'Am I...?' she asked, unable to finish the question. Because, if she was pregnant, she'd just driven away the baby's father with her selfish need for love—as well as destroying the future of her country.

Claire nodded.

The room spun and Kaliana couldn't focus on anything. Blackness, darker than the night sky, swirled around her, making standing up almost impossible. She wanted to give into it. Wanted the darkness to sweep her away. Take her somewhere she didn't have to think. Somewhere she could be alone with the knowledge that she carried Rafe's baby inside her. Somewhere she could be free of the pain of loving a man who would never love her.

Rafe strode into the room he'd been shown to. He hadn't even wanted to see Kaliana's father first. All he'd wanted was her. The doors closed behind him but Kaliana wasn't in the room. Only Claire.

'Where is she?' he demanded as Claire stood up to greet him, thankful that Kaliana's friend had been just that, with her parting advice to him as she'd left Villa Casella only hours after Kaliana.

'Don't give up on love, Rafe—or Kaliana.'

He could still hear her saying those words as the quiet of the house had shrouded them after the guests had gone. He had no idea what Claire had meant and had pushed that sentimental bit of advice to the back of his mind as he'd dealt with his business matters.

But he'd kept hearing it. Over and over. And then he'd known with such absolute certainty it was like standing under an icy shower. He loved Kaliana and if he loved her he needed to set her free from their deal. Give her the freedom to choose who she married. Who she loved. Then hope it would be him.

His business deals had quickly taken second place to negotiations with her father as the two men reached an agreement which financially secured the kingdom of Ardu Safra but meant Kaliana didn't have to marry—him or Nassif—to do that. Just as that had fallen into place Enzo had come to him, telling him about his reconciliation with Emma after news from his lawyer regarding the Casella inheritance. News that freed both Kaliana and himself from their deal in a way he'd never envisaged possible. Once all that was secured, Rafe had left Sicily for Ardu Safra. For Kaliana.

One final meeting with legal teams last night had secured the deal Kaliana's father and he had agreed on. Her father hadn't asked why, but Rafe suspected he knew. Damn it. It seemed everyone knew that he loved Kaliana.

Except Kaliana herself. Something he intended to put right.

'What do you want, Rafe?' Kaliana's voice seemed to tremble even though her expression was firm and strong, but she looked so pale as she came into the room and sat down. Was she ill?

Rafe frowned, moving closer to the woman he loved, but she didn't look up at him. That welcome smile he'd imagined would be on her face wasn't there. She couldn't look at him.

'What's wrong?' When Kaliana didn't answer he looked to Claire.

'I'll leave you both to talk,' Claire said, walking away. Rafe watched her leave the room, even though he suspected she knew what was wrong. He turned his attention back to Kaliana. To her pale cheeks and the telltale darkness beneath her eyes. She'd had as little sleep as he'd had. Did she regret walking away? Was there one last ray of hope for him, for them? He'd come here hoping to find it—and the strength to admit what he felt for her. To admit he loved her.

Rafe waited as Claire's retreating footsteps quietened to nothing, the silence in the cool marble room almost screaming at him. Its heaviness filled with uncertainty.

Kaliana stood up, moving towards him slowly, her face so very pale. Her eyes full of sadness. 'Why are you here, Rafe?'

Her question confused him, but he couldn't help his gaze slipping down over her. He'd never seen her dressed in anything so beautiful as the pale blue silk which wound its way around her body, accentuating and yet concealing it. She looked regal. Elegant in the dress of her country. It was as if he was truly seeing her for the first time as a princess. Which made what he'd come here to do, to say, even more important.

'We need to talk.' He saw her lips pressing together, as if she was fighting to hold back her words. 'We need to talk about our deal. Our marriage deal.'

She looked down, becoming even paler. 'Yes, Rafe, we do.' There was resignation in her voice. He didn't want her to resign herself to marriage to him. If they married, it had to be for one reason only. But where did he begin? He couldn't just blurt out that he loved her. After that staunch denial about his ability to love anyone. She'd think it was the deal, his need to marry and produce an heir which drove him.

'When you left Villa Casella, I was sure it was over. Certain you didn't want to marry anyone. Not Nassif. And not me.' He injected firm determination into his voice. The revelations of the last few days, days which had kept him from coming to Ardu Safra, had fuelled that determination. He wasn't about to allow her to walk away from him yet. Not until she knew everything.

Kaliana's breath was dragged in on a ragged inhale, her nervousness all too clear. 'Want isn't part of it, Rafe. We both know that.' She moved away from him, sitting in the seat set beneath the windows, the view of her country spreading out behind her reminding him of who she was. Her eyes were full of sadness as she looked up at him. 'I made a deal, Rafe. A deal I have to keep—for my country's sake, my people's sake, I have to keep that deal. I have to marry.'

'I am here to free you of that deal, that marriage.' He stood firm against the shock rushing over her face. The same shock he'd felt surge through him when he'd realised there was a way out—for both of them. A way for them to be free to explore their love.

Her brows furrowed in confusion. 'How?' She breathed the word as if grasping onto a lifeline, confirming everything she'd led him to believe before she'd left Villa Casella. She didn't want marriage. Because she was still in love with Alif, the man fate had snatched away from her.

'I have put a deal to your father, one that will help the country's finances and give you the time you need.' Her father had needed little persuading. It seemed he knew, even accepted, that deep down his daughter had no wish for marriage.

She blinked rapidly, sitting up quickly, dragging in a breath and pressing her fingers to her forehead, her face paling. He moved towards her, unable to help himself. Crouching down in front of her, he looked into those gorgeous brown eyes. 'Are you unwell?'

'No.' The word shot from her and she pulled back. 'I just don't understand. Why would you do that? Why would my father even accept it?' She looked up at him. 'Why didn't he say anything to me?'

'I asked him not to.' That got her attention. 'I wanted to tell you myself. Face to face.'

'Then you had better tell me. Everything.' She trembled, looking even paler, and again he worried that she was ill. 'Tell me, Rafe.'

'Your father and I have struck a deal, on the understanding that you do not have to marry at all. The finances of the country are now settled and the pressure off.'

'How?' Her delicate brows furrowed into a frown of disbelief. 'How are they settled?'

'I'm financing the deal.' He didn't want to go into details now. Not when he needed other details. Emotional details.

'Why would you do that?'

'I know you loved Alif. I know you believe you will never find that love again.'

He paused as she looked at him, her head tilting to one side, pain in her eyes, in every line of her frown. 'I did love him,' she whispered as she looked down at her hands, tightly knotted in her lap.

'I know,' he said, lifting her chin up, needing to see her face, her eyes. 'Now you are free to find real love. To marry for love.'

'What about the baby?' The words shuddered from her on a sob. One that was racked with pain.

'The baby?' For a moment everything stopped. The baby he'd needed but hadn't wanted. Now, just like his feelings for this woman, all that had changed. He did want to be a father. But only if this woman agreed to be his wife. And only when she could love him. However long that took.

'You are the only male Casella able to continue the family. You *need* a baby. A son.' There was a hint of hysteria in her voice and he sat next to her, taking her clasped hands between his.

'So much has changed since that night at Villa Casella. Emma…' he began but Kaliana pulled her hands back so quickly the words dried up. Even now, he couldn't believe what he'd learnt about his brother's marriage, or that his father was happy with it.

'You are in love with Emma, I know.' Ice slipped into her words. Her eyes.

Rafe looked down. Damn it, he should have been more honest with Kaliana. More open. Maybe then she'd have seen that the pain of Emma's rejection was keeping him from falling in love with her.

He took a deep breath, looking at her, willing her to understand. 'I was in love with Emma, but not any more. Now I love her as a friend. A sister-in-law. My brother's wife. The woman who, with her husband, my twin brother, is planning to adopt.'

A wave of nausea rushed over Kaliana and she placed her palm over her stomach. Over the baby she and Rafe had created with such passion. The baby he no longer wanted—or needed. The baby he'd done a deal with her father to avoid having. Panic rushed through her and she grasped at anything.

'What about the Casella heir? The next generation.'

He smiled at her, breaking her heart with the kindness she saw in his eyes. 'Enzo's lawyers have found one small loophole in the inheritance terms. So long as Enzo and Emma officially adopt, that child will be able to inherit. My father is more than happy with that news. As am I.'

He still crouched in front of her, looking at her with concern on his face, as if he knew she was worried about something. She looked into the darkness of his eyes and a smile slipped, weakly and involuntarily, to her lips. 'You'll be an uncle.'

He looked at her, his gaze steady and firm, holding her prisoner. '*Sì*, I will be an uncle. And, thanks to you, to the effort you went to, encouraging me to reach out to Enzo, I now have my brother back.'

'I wish you'd introduced me properly to Emma.' The words lurched from her as she searched his face.

'I should have,' he said, looking down briefly before looking back up into her eyes. The barriers he'd always locked himself behind were down. She could see beyond them. Could she reach the man she loved if she tried? 'I don't know why I didn't.'

But if she didn't reach him… The thought of rejection kept her silent.

'Maybe because our relationship was just pretence. Because our emotions weren't involved.' He shrugged as if it didn't matter. But it did. It mattered because she loved him.

'What happens now you've made this deal with my father and the Casella heir is secured?' She shocked herself at how business-like her voice sounded. How calm.

'We are both free of the obligations of our deal. We no longer need to marry.' His jaw was pressed firmly together, and his eyes hardened. He was waiting for her to agree. Waiting for her to free him.

'Then there will be no wedding,' she said, more to herself than Rafe, her mind drifting off with the secret of the baby she carried. Rafe's baby. She didn't want to be set free, but if she told him now? He'd think she wanted him just because of the baby. She looked at him, trying to read his mind. Trying to guess what he wanted. 'And no need to have a baby.'

'No. The deal is off. And one day, when you find love again, you will look back on this moment and thank me.' He stood up. That was it? He was walking out on her.

She dragged in a breath and the words almost tumbled out, but she stopped them. How could she tell him she loved him now? That she'd already found that love? A deep and meaningful love she'd never felt for Alif. How could she say that it didn't matter what deal was on—or off—she *wanted* to be his wife?

Because she loved him.

She pushed her fingers into her hair. She couldn't tell him that, couldn't open her heart to more pain. But she had to tell him about the baby. Whatever else happened, he had a right to know.

'It's really good that everything is sorted, that you and Enzo are friends again, and that everyone lives happily ever after.' She dragged her hands down through her hair, clutching at the ends of it as if it were her lifeline, looking at him, hating how what she had to say would change everything. 'But there is one problem.'

'Problem?' His eyes narrowed in suspicion.

She lifted her chin determinedly, looking

into his eyes, into the darkness that had so often been filled with desire for her. Now they were clouded with something which broke her heart. Fear. Already it seemed he was drawing away from her. He'd made a deal with her father simply to enable him to walk away from her, their engagement. Would he walk away from their child too?

'What problem, Kaliana?' Rafe asked firmly.

She just had to say it. There was no easy way. She took a deep breath, letting it go, looking directly into his eyes. 'I'm pregnant.'

The floor dropped from beneath Rafe's feet. Or at least that was how it felt. Kaliana was pregnant. With his child.

He'd thought he'd got it all sorted. Thought he was doing the right thing—for Kaliana— the woman he loved. He'd thought he was setting her free. She still loved Alif and he couldn't compete with a man who wasn't able to stand there and face him. Not that he'd been able to compete with Enzo, but this was different. This was real. His love for Kaliana was real and he couldn't compete with the memory of Alif. For her love. He had to let her go. Set her free to make her own choices. If what they'd shared since that first night in London meant something to her, there was a chance she might choose him.

He'd intended to stand back and wait, allow her time to adjust to her freedom from the need to marry anyone. But now? Everything had changed. All he'd sorted with Enzo and Emma, with his father and Kaliana's father, had all been in vain.

Kaliana was having his child. A child he didn't even know if he could be a good father to. His doubts crept in like a dark shadow. He'd done it all wrong, let Kaliana down.

'Rafe?' Kaliana questioned, dragging him brutally from his thoughts, pain and fear in her voice. Damn it, he wouldn't let her down. He wouldn't.

'Pregnant?' It was all he could say. He couldn't move to her, couldn't take her in his arms and tell her it would all be okay even though he wanted to. Because he didn't know if he could make this okay. He wanted to tell her he loved her, wanted her to tell him the same.

She was carrying his child. He had to marry her now. He couldn't live with himself if he turned his back on her—on his baby. After a fleeting glimpse of freedom, they were now back where they'd started.

'There was that one night,' she said in a whisper. 'We woke and made love...' She left the rest of the explanation unsaid and memories of that night rushed back at him, of how it had felt to make her his without anything between them. For that short time, he'd been certain there hadn't been any emotional barriers and neither had there been any physical ones.

'Without any protection.' He inhaled deeply. Damn it. This was his fault. He should have protected her, protected them both. Whatever the mood of the moment, he should have protected her. Once again, he'd failed.

She closed her eyes. 'Yes.' Her pained whisper slashed at his heart.

He walked towards her, wanting to reach for her, wanting to hold her, to inhale the scent of her hair as he pressed a kiss onto her head, but her rigid regal stance warned him off. 'This changes things.'

She sighed, a look of resignation sweeping into her eyes, taking the sparkle from them. The sparkle he loved so much. 'I thought it might.'

He searched her face, desperate for a hint of something more than resignation. But nothing. Cool, regal indifference shone back at him from her eyes. He knew, just as she did, that as Princess of Ardu Safra she couldn't be an unmarried mother.

'You can't expect me to turn my back on my child and I'm certain that your father will not tolerate you raising his heir alone. Unmarried. There is only one thing we can do and that is to marry as arranged.'

She looked up at him slowly, as if she couldn't believe what he was saying. 'What about the deal with my father?'

Was that all she could think of? Pain slashed at him like a whip to his flesh. If she had any feelings for him, if she had even the smallest bit of love for him, wouldn't she say it? 'I will honour my deal with your father, just as I will honour my duty to you—and my baby.'

His annoyance at himself, at falling in love—again—with a woman who didn't love him back drove him on, made his words sharp and brittle.

'No.' She backed away from him. 'No, Rafe. I can't marry you.'

'Can't or won't?' The question snapped from him like a firecracker.

'Both.'

He looked at her, seeing the pain in her eyes, in the furrows of her forehead, in the single tear which had slipped from her eye to run down her pale cheek. His heart wrenched. His gut clenched.

'Kaliana, the baby.' He could scarcely breathe. He was losing Kaliana—losing the woman he loved—and he didn't know how to stop it happening.

'When I saw you with Emma...' Kaliana looked down as if afraid to speak, then she looked back up, full of confidence, full of fire '... I knew we couldn't marry. I knew I'd have to return to Ardu Safra and marry

Nassif. The deal you've made with my father will save me from that and I appreciate it, but the baby makes no difference. I can't marry you.'

'You appreciate what I have done?' What the hell was going on? Where was the woman who'd loved with passionate abandon in Rome? The woman who'd brought him slowly but surely from the darkness he'd been in since losing Emma? He'd been too stubborn to hold onto Kaliana at the party, to tell her then what he felt, and that stubbornness had given her the chance to walk away from him.

She reached out, placing her hand on his arm. 'Yes, Rafe. For that I am so grateful, but I can't marry you. Now more than ever.'

He drew in a sharp breath, turning from her, striding to the other window, looking out at a landscape that was so alien to him. As alien as the love which filled his heart—for a woman who didn't want him. Didn't love him.

He clenched his jaw as her words replayed in his mind, finally able to form his own words. 'Why not? You are carrying my baby! You are a princess. You can't have a baby alone.'

'I can have this baby alone and I will. I want to marry for love, Rafe.' Her voice was like a strangled cry and he turned to face her, the distance between them small but insurmountable. 'Not because of a deal. Or the baby. I want to marry for love.'

'Love?'

'Yes. I want the man I marry to love me. I want to marry him for no other reason than he loves me.'

'You don't want to be loved, Kaliana. You've had your love. Isn't that what you told me?' Anger surged through Rafe. Anger for a man who'd made it impossible to reach the woman he loved. Or had that man been him? He had to put his heart on the line, tell her he'd fallen in love with her, deeper, harder than he'd ever loved any woman. But how could he when she was still in love with Alif?

'We are good together. We had something special.' Desperation and frustration fuelled his words like nothing he'd ever known. 'You can't walk away from that, just as I can't walk away from the duty to my child.'

CHAPTER TEN

KALIANA COULDN'T UNDERSTAND what Rafe was saying. First, he'd told her she was free of their deal. That he'd made arrangements with her father, a deal which meant she didn't have to marry anyone. The pain of realising he'd done that because he didn't want to go through with their marriage slashed at her face like tiny grains of sand in a cruel desert wind.

He'd made that deal because he didn't want to marry her. Didn't want to have children. Now that she'd told him she was carrying his child, he was telling her she couldn't walk away. She dragged in a sharp breath of despair. How could he say she didn't want love after everything they'd shared, all those passionate nights in Rome?

Because, for him, each time they'd made

love had been nothing more than lust and desire. He hadn't felt love growing for her as she had for him.

She pressed her fingertips to her forehead, inhaling deeply, nausea battling with confusion and heartbreak. 'I do want love, Rafe. I want to be loved, but for me, because of who I am, not anything I can give a man.'

She turned her back on him. This was pointless and she couldn't bear the anger in his eyes. Her heart was breaking, and he'd done little to heal it since he'd arrived. If anything, he'd made it worse. It was duty which forced him to tell her she couldn't walk away from him. Duty to his unborn baby. The child he didn't want.

'You've shut love out of your life, and I get that.' She spoke more calmly now, but she couldn't look at him. Couldn't bear to see the annoyance on his face.

'But, unlike you, I'm beginning to realise I can't shut it out. That I want to be loved. That I want to love.' The admission was torn from her in a tortured whisper.

She could feel him moving closer. Feel it

with every nerve in her body, but she still couldn't look at him. Silence lingered, tense and full of expectation. Her breathing was rapid and shallow as she waited for him to speak. Waited for him to tell her again that he couldn't love anyone.

'Then don't walk away from me, Kaliana. Don't shut me out.' His voice had become a hoarse whisper, full of pleading. She frowned, unable to turn to him, unable to allow the small glimmer of hope to spark into something bigger. Something that would let her down. Break her heart. 'Look at me, Kaliana. Look at me.'

She took a deep breath, turning to face him. In just a few minutes his expression had changed. Gone from that of a man totally sure of himself to a man walking into territory he'd never explored. An expression of uncertainty.

That glimmer of hope inside her flickered, rising a little higher.

'You are the one who has only just arrived here, Rafe. You are the one who has been absent, without even a message, for the last five days.' She couldn't allow herself to hope. Couldn't allow herself to read more into this. 'What else am I supposed to think after our conversation, other than you don't want our deal? Don't want me.'

'I couldn't come to you.'

'Or even send a message? Call me?'

'That is what lovers would do.' There was a trace of shame in his voice. 'And we are not lovers.'

Anger surged forward, making her thoughts irrational. 'We were portraying lovers.'

Rafe drew in a long deep breath. 'I was setting the deal up with your father so that you didn't have to marry me—or Nassif. I had nothing to tell you. But it seems you had plenty to tell me.'

'It was only this morning I knew for certain about the baby,' she defended herself hotly. How dare he turn this on her? 'You could have told me what you were doing, Rafe. I could have spoken with my father.'

'I wanted to present you with a done deal.' He moved a little closer and her heart hammered in her chest. 'I wanted to set you free.'

The flicker of hope dimmed. 'I could never marry Nassif,' she whispered.

He moved, the light from the sun streaming in behind him, leaving him in the shadow of the thick palace walls, reminding her of their last conversation in Villa Casella. 'I know.' His expression hardened slightly. Or was it the shadows? 'Just as I know you can't marry me, but we have made a baby together, Kaliana. A child. A child that changes everything. Even the deal you put to me in Palermo. The baby changes everything.'

'Yes,' she breathed. 'The baby changes everything.'

'So, what is the problem, *cara mia*?' Why did he have to call her that? Why did he have to soften her now? When she was trying to be so strong. What would he do if she told him the truth? Told him she loved him.

'I loved Alif,' she said, suddenly needing to explain it all. Tell him everything which she'd kept hidden—even from herself. 'I loved him so much.'

He nodded. 'I know. And you lost him and believe love will never be yours again, that you don't deserve it.' The impassioned words rushed from him and she frowned. He'd never been this emotional before. Practical. Strong and resilient. But never emotional. The barriers around his emotions had never lifted like this. She could see it in his eyes. Hear it in his voice. He was letting her in, so shouldn't she allow him past her barriers?

'I did believe that,' she said softly, unable to help herself from walking to him, the need to be closer to him, to see if she could cross through that barrier around him too great. 'Until a few weeks ago.'

He looked into her eyes, the darkness of his filled with concern. Confusion. 'What happened a few weeks ago?'

He had no idea. No idea she'd fallen in love with him. That every caress, every kiss they'd shared in Rome had come from her heart. That every time they'd made love she'd fallen a little more in love with him. But then, she hadn't even seen it herself. She'd tried valiantly to deny it.

Could she tell him? She looked into his eyes, seeing them bare of that barrier. If she didn't tell him now she would have to walk away and never look back. Never wonder *What if?*

'I fell in love.'

The air stilled around them, as if the soft wind of the desert had eased, waiting to see what would happen. The heat became even more oppressive as his eyes held hers, going deep into her soul. Her heart.

'Fell in love?' The deep and husky whisper reminded her of how his voice sounded after they made love. When he held her in his arms, making her feel as if she was the most precious thing in the world.

'With you, Rafe,' she whispered, holding that electrifying connection between them, not daring to let it break. If she did, she might never get this chance again. Never be able to slip beyond those barriers and barricades. 'I fell in love with you.'

For the second time in as many minutes the floor dropped away from beneath Rafe's feet. The world lurched and spun. Kaliana loved him? The woman he loved, the woman for whom he'd changed everything to enable her to have the freedom to live and love as she wanted, loved him? The woman who was carrying his child.

But could he believe it? Could he allow himself to hope, when she'd just told him she was expecting his child? He hated himself for doubting her, but what if she was just saying it because of the baby?

'Why did you walk away from me the night of our engagement party?' The hurt from that night, the pain of believing that he didn't deserve her love, rushed forward, making every word he spoke sound bitter.

'I saw the way you looked at Emma.' Kaliana's voice was as brittle as ice, her eyes full of fear, pain. 'I saw the way you touched her, Rafe, and I guess I made my own deductions.'

Kaliana looked down, a blush rushing prettily over her face, and he smiled. He shouldn't be happy with that explanation, with that reaction, but he was. It proved she felt something for him. Proved it was deep enough for her to be put out, even jealous, of the friendship he and Emma had carved out of the mess that was their brief love affair.

'I loved Emma once,' he said, his heart flooding with hope as she looked up at him, pain in her eyes, her expression. 'But now only as a friend. A sister. I'm happy for her—and for Enzo. Happy they are making a go of their marriage, that they are adopting a child. Emma always wanted to be a mother. Enzo felt he'd failed Emma, so did everything he could to push her away. But their love was too strong.'

It was a trait he shared, he acknowledged, looking at Kaliana, her expression changing as she processed all he'd told her. All he should have told her long ago.

'And the child they adopt will be enough to save the Casella inheritance? Save the family name?' She moved a little closer, as if she couldn't help herself. As if she too was hanging onto a fragile thread of hope.

He took her hands in his, keeping her close. 'Yes, their child will become the next Casella to inherit the family fortune.'

'So you really don't need to marry me?'

Her voice wobbled, her eyes filled with un-shed tears and his heart broke. The heart that loved her so much. 'Or have a child?'

'No, I don't.' Her shoulders dropped and her hands felt limp within his. 'But I want to. I want to marry you.'

She shook her head, the denial confusing him, knocking down the confidence to say those three words aloud. To tell her he loved her. 'Just because I'm pregnant? I can't, Rafe.' She pulled her hands free of his, pain in her voice. He had to tell her, had to knock that final barrier down before he lost her for good.

'Kaliana, stop,' he said, gently holding her face between his hands, looking deep into her eyes.

She closed her eyes. Shut him out. Damn it, he wasn't going to be beaten. She couldn't keep him locked out like this—when he'd dismantled almost every barricade he'd ever erected. But there was one more remaining. The one which kept him from saying he loved her. The one he intended to obliterate right now.

'Kaliana, look at me.' He breathed her name

in a whisper, waiting until she opened her eyes, needing her to see the love for her in his. 'I love you, Kaliana. I want you to be my wife. I want you to be the mother of my children.'

Kaliana looked at Rafe, unable to think, to speak—or even breathe. He loved her? He'd spent the last five days ensuring she could be free of the need to marry anyone. Because he loved her.

She placed her hands either side of his face, mirroring his need to hold her, make her look at him, see deep into his eyes. Beneath her fingers she felt the uncustomary hardness of his stubble. She smiled and took a deep breath, inhaling the evocative scent that was Rafe. The man she loved. The man who had just admitted to loving her.

'You set me free? Because you love me?' she whispered, moving so close she could almost press her lips to his. Almost kiss him. And she wanted to, so much.

'*Sì...*' He stumbled from Italian to English.

'Yes, I love you, but I want you to be happy— even if that isn't with me.'

'The only way I can ever be happy is with you, Rafe.' She looked into his eyes, saw the questions slip away, saw the sparks of happiness brushing them aside. Slowly she pressed her lips to his, closing her eyes as that contact sparked the usual fireworks in her body.

When he kissed her back a tear sprang from beneath her eyelid, rushing down her cheek, wetting his. He moved back, looking intently at her.

'You are crying.'

'Tears of happiness,' she said as another tear tumbled down her cheek. 'I have everything I could ever want. A man who loves me, a man I love with all my heart, and his baby.'

He kissed her cheek, catching the next tear. 'I love you, Kaliana. So very much. Will you make me the happiest man alive and marry me?'

She laughed as another tear tumbled down her cheek. 'I will, but you don't have to do it here, in Ardu Safra, or so soon.'

'I'm not waiting any longer than I need to

wait to make you my wife.' He gave her that suggestive flick of his brows, sending heat spiralling through her. She pressed herself closer to him, sliding her hands around his neck. She loved him so much and if she could marry him right now, right this minute, she would.

'The wedding preparations are all made. Everything is in place for us to marry. Is two weeks too long?' she teased as her fingers slid into the thickness of his hair.

'Far too long.' He kissed her gently, holding her closer still to him, so that she could feel every contour of his body. Feel the need he had for her right now. 'But waiting two weeks to spend the rest of my life with you will be worth it.'

'I love you, Rafe.' She breathed the words she'd longed to say since the night in Rome when their baby had been conceived.

'And I love you, Kaliana, and I intend to spend the rest of my life showing you just how much. Each and every single day.' He kissed her, deeper and harder than he'd ever kissed her, and Kaliana knew they had both broken down the barriers which had entrapped them since their first unlucky encounters with love. They'd both left the shadows of darkness, coming out into the brightness of love.

EPILOGUE

THE EARLY SUMMER sunshine bathed the gardens of Villa Casella in a golden glow as the sun began to set. The garden was filled with friends and family who'd come to welcome the arrival of the next Casella generation. Rafe's father took every opportunity to spend time with his ever-expanding family. Even Kaliana's mother and father had travelled from Ardu Safra for the party and from the smile on her mother's face Kaliana was certain she enjoyed being a grandmother. Her father, of course, tried very hard to remain serious, but to no avail. Little Paulo had quite literally got him dancing to his tune.

'Paulo is utterly gorgeous,' Kaliana said as she sat watching the toddler Emma and Enzo had adopted, their adoration and love for each other and the little boy obvious for all to see. Their happiness at finally being a family filled Kaliana with joy whenever she thought of where they'd all been this time last year.

Rafe leant forwards, kissing her cheek softly. 'It's hard to believe that a year ago there were no future Casella heirs. Now there's a whole new generation.'

Kaliana glanced at the baby monitor on the table next to her iced lemonade, still unable to believe she was a mother. The mother of a beautiful baby girl and a handsome baby boy. 'I'm looking forward to Lorenzo and Layla being able to toddle around the garden like Paulo.'

Rafe laughed softly, love shining from his eyes as he looked at her. 'Be prepared for them to be a real handful.' He sat back next to her, his long legs stretching out before him, unfurling that ever-constant need she had for him. 'My mother always said that's exactly what Enzo and I were. A handful.'

Kaliana laughed. 'You still are, both of you.'

'That is not fair.' His voice was mockingly

stern, the sparkle of love brighter than ever in his eyes.

'Maybe a boy and a girl will be different.' The love she felt for Rafe, for her babies, filled every word as she looked at him, always ready to tease him a little.

Baby snuffling noises sounded on the monitor and they both looked at it, smiling. 'If Layla is anything like her mother, then it will be because poor little Lorenzo will be continually bossed and teased by his big sister.'

'Are you saying I boss you around?' She sat forwards, leaning into him and brushing her lips over his. 'Tease maybe, but not boss.'

'I like a strong woman,' he said, pulling her onto his lap and kissing her, oblivious and uncaring of their guests. 'But, more than anything else, I love you. My strong woman. The mother of my beautiful twins.'

'And I love the man I married, the father of my babies. I love you to the point of distraction.'

She closed her eyes and he kissed her, hard and passionately. When he ceased the torment, pulling back from her, she could see the love in his eyes and smiled. She was happy, loved and in love—far more than she'd ever dared to hope for that night she'd walked into the hotel bar in London.

'I love you, Kaliana. With all my heart and every day I love you a little deeper. You are my world.'

* * * * *

LET'S TALK

Romance

For exclusive extracts, competitions and special offers, find us online:

facebook.com/millsandboon

@millsandboonuk

@millsandboon

Or get in touch on 0844 844 1351*

For all the latest titles coming soon, visit millsandboon.co.uk/nextmonth